THE COWBOY &
EMILY TIPTON

SHARON KIZZIAH-HOLMES

Publishing Coordinator – Sharon Kizziah-Holmes
Cover Design – Sweet n Spicy Designs

Paperback-Press
an imprint of A & S Publishing
A & S Holmes, Inc.

ISBN -13: 978-1-945669-95-8

DEDICATION

To my granddaughters who's names are in the story. I love each and every one of you.

Love, Gado

ACKNOWLEDGMENTS

A special thank you to Kathleen Garnsey, Tierney James, Susan Keene and Shirley McCann. You ladies are awesome! I couldn't do anything without your support in all that I do. Friends like you are what life's about.

To Jaycee DeLorenzo with Sweet 'n Spicy Designs, this cover is perfect. I love it!

Husband, all I can say is thank you for always standing beside me through life. Also, thanks for supporting my writing and publishing efforts. I appreciate you more than you know.

Last but not least, thank you Ozarks Romance Authors for helping me start my writing career so many years ago. Still today you're here for me any time I call upon you.

CHAPTER ONE

Emily?"

Emily Tipton glanced in the direction of her Aunt Ruby's voice. "In the study, Auntie." The buxom lady who'd raised her entered the room.

"Look what just came in the mail."

She studied the envelope her aunt handed her. "Auntie, this is from Kail, Cooper and Mills in Dallas." Her heart pounded. Was it an acceptance of her application for a job as a legal secretary? Or was it another, 'sorry, the position's been filled'?

"Well, don't just sit there staring at it, open it and see what they say."

Emily swallowed the lump in her throat and said a silent prayer. This was truly the job she wanted, even though she'd sent apps to other prospects. She held the letter and stared at the creased paper while her pulse raced.

"Why are you stalling?"

"I'm afraid they didn't hire me."

"Well, you'll never know unless you unfold that and read it."

Her aunt was right. She'd have to look sooner or later. She opened the top fold, then the bottom, noting the gold embossed personalized letterhead. She cleared her throat to steady her voice. "Dear Miss Tipton," she read. "We are pleased to inform you that the legal secretarial position at Kail, Cooper and Mills, is yours." She sprang from her chair, ran around the desk and gave Ruby Collins a bear hug. "I got it! I got the job!"

Ruby laughed. "Indeed you did." She pushed Emily to arm's length. "Now, read the rest and let's hear what else they have to say."

She scanned the page. "You will start on June first." That was only forty-five days away.

"Our company will pay all of your moving expenses; the deposit and first month's rent on an apartment or house of your choice and give you a month's pay to help with other costs that might incur." She glanced up. "Did you hear that?"

Ruby smiled. "It's more than generous. They must want you badly, dear."

"It sounds like it, doesn't it?" She met the gaze of the woman she loved with all her heart. "You're coming with me, aren't you?" The look in Ruby's eyes gave her answer.

"No, my life is here in Lubbock. You go on to Dallas and start your new life."

"But what if Unc—"

"He's not coming back." Ruby shook her head. "Your uncle Abe is long gone and has been for over fifteen years. We sold the ranch, and I'm sure he hasn't thought about us since. I'll be fine."

Her aunt was right. Dreams of finding an apartment in Dallas, starting a new job and beginning her professional life filled her heart with joy. Had her father not abandoned her and her mother, and Uncle Able not been so abusive, she might think about settling down and having children of her own, but she would have no part of it. Those two men stomped on her heart and she'd vowed never to fall in love. A man would only hurt her or leave her.

Her thoughts went to her old friend Randle. She *did* trust him, but with friendship, not with her heart. Why couldn't he have been someone she looked at through different eyes? There just wasn't the attraction of a lover.

A twenty-four-year-old virgin. How sad, but she'd lived with it this long and would continue to live with it. Why was she even thinking about this now? She had the job of her dreams and it was time for a little happiness in her life. "Auntie, I'm goin' to Dallas!"

~ ~ ~

Emily unlocked the door to her new loft apartment and stepped inside. She loved her job, her new bosses, her new everything. Life was good. She tossed her purse and keys on the entry hall table and went to her bedroom to prepare a hot bath, the perfect thing to begin her weekend. She kicked off her shoes and started to remove her suit jacket when she noticed something amiss in her room.

A shiver ran down her spine. Had someone been in there? She'd made her bed before she left that morning, but not quite as perfect as it now appeared. She scanned the room. Who would be able to get in? This was something her aunt would do after Emily left in the mornings, but Ruby wasn't here.

She strolled through the rest of the spacious loft. Nothing else seemed out of the ordinary. She shrugged and realized maybe she was getting in the 'mighty tidy' mode her aunt had been in for the last few years. Of course, how silly to think someone had been inside. She'd become more organized and did it without thinking. To be on the safe side, before she went in for her bath, she made sure both locks on the door were secure.

Settling back into the oversized tub, she began to relax. This place was a lot different than the small apartment she and Aunt Ruby moved into years ago. She had never been so glad to get away from cowboys and horses in her life than she was when Ruby divorced Able Collins's abusive ass and left the ranch.

She wanted to think about something else. Something that made her happy. Her new life in Dallas.

In the past two months, she'd learned a lot about the city. She was lucky her aunt knew the Meyers, the nice older couple who owned the loft apartments. Emily was thrilled to find out they had an opening. But the big plus was that the apartment was only a fifteen-minute drive from work.

The ring of her cell phone across the room caught her attention. The last thing she wanted to do was jump out of the warm comfort of the water to answer it, but what if it was an emergency? A towel lay close to the tub. She grabbed it, stood, then wrapped it around her.

The moment she reached for the cell it stopped ringing. She checked the caller ID. Brittany Mills? Why would her boss's daughter be calling? She worked with her at the office, but they had never been social. The beep notified her Brittany had left a message. She dialed her voicemail and listened.

"Hi, Emily, this is Brittany. Hey, it's Friday night and I'm going out with some friends, thought you might want to go. Give me a callback. Hope you decide to, it'll be fun. 555-6398. Later."

She hadn't gone anywhere, but grocery shopping, work and home since she moved to Dallas. Maybe a night on the town would be fun. She liked Brittany. However, she'd brought some work home from the office, and that needed to be done. She should probably just stay in. After drying off, she put on her robe, grabbed the phone and dialed Brittany back. On the third ring, she answered.

"Hello."

"Hi, this is Emily. You called?"

"Yeah, I'm going to dinner with a couple more girls and wanted to see if you'd like to join us."

"Well, I've been thinking about it and I don't know. I really need to get some files straightened out that I brought home from work."

"Are you crazy? Work on the weekends? How boring! You need to get a life, Emily. Come on and go with us. I'll pick you up."

It was pretty bad when a co-worker related you to the word boring. What the heck. It couldn't hurt anything and she'd have the rest of the weekend to work. She took a deep breath and squared her shoulders. "Ok, I'll go." She had to hold the phone away from her ear when she heard Brittany screech her words out in a high pitched shrill voice.

"Yipeeeeeee. You won't regret it. I promise."

Somehow, *she* wasn't as sure as Brittany sounded.

CHAPTER TWO

Cigarette smoke cast a haze through the dim light of the country nightclub. Music blared from the stage as the band played *Johnny B. Goode*. The last place Zeb wanted to be was at The Hitchin' Post on a Friday night. He'd rather be back at the ranch taking a late evening horseback ride. However, when a clue led him somewhere, he had to check it out. Being a cowboy made it easy for him to fit in.

He'd spent enough time there in his younger days, drinking beer and dancing a two-step or waltz with the pretty girls. It used to be his main hang before he met Jasmine, the love of his life, during a traffic stop. The woman he'd planned to marry.

Being a Texas Ranger seemed like a lifetime ago when in reality it had been only eighteen months. No! He refused to let himself think about that part of his past. He was glad those days were over. Glad he was no longer in law enforcement. After all that time, he was still trying to convince himself of that. One day, maybe he'd believe it.

The booth in the back corner was the perfect place to scope out everyone who entered. One thing he'd learned as a former Texas State Trooper, then a Texas Ranger, before he became a private investigator, was to keep his back to the wall.

The door opened and his suspicions were confirmed. His client's husband entered with a sweet young thing on his arm. Was the man stupid? Didn't he know a good woman was something to cherish? This man had three children at home and a wife who adored him. Now look at the mess he was making of his life. All for a fling with a bimbo he'd never leave his family for. But now it was too late. Tomorrow, his life would change forever.

He reached to his belt, flipped open the leather case and pulled out the low-light camcorder/camera, which looked like a pager. Domestics weren't his favorites, but it was a steady source of income whether he liked it or not.

However, it was his job. He downed what was left of his beer, got up and started for the exit. Just as he pushed at the door, it swung open. Two young women stood on the other side. He was surprised he knew one of them. He had grown up with her. "Howdy, Brittany." He stepped aside so they could enter. After he introduced Brittany to his fiancée a few years back, the women had become best friends.

"Hey, Zeb, you're not leaving are you?"

"Yeah. My work here is done."

"Work my foot. You're here looking for some pretty girls to dance with and we just showed up."

Dancing wasn't on his mind until he saw the beautiful woman with Brittany. Her dark chestnut hair shined with soft red highlights, even in the dimness of the club lighting. "You think so?"

"Yes, I do, so come on, let's get a table."

His gaze held that of the intriguing woman with his old friend, and for a moment his heart threatened to stop. In law enforcement, he'd learned to read people pretty well. This woman's gorgeous green eyes were cautious, maybe even somewhat afraid, as she quickly glanced away and studied the bar room. Was she scared of something? Maybe it was just the place. She didn't look like the type to frequent taverns like The Hitchin' Post, but as the saying went, you can't judge a book by its cover.

Brittany clasped his hand. He hoped she didn't want to play the 'matchmaking game' with him again. The last thing he wanted, or needed, was a woman in his life. Not this soon.

"Have you met Emily yet?"

Emily, what a pretty name. "No, can't say I have." But no matter how hard he fought it, he wanted to.

"Emily Tipton, this is Zebulon, but everyone calls him Zeb. He's one of the most available men in Dallas. However, he swears he's not looking."

He glanced at Brittany, raised a warning eyebrow at her then focused back on Emily. "Howdy, ma'am. Nice to meet you."

"Well, what are we waiting for?" Brittany tugged

Zeb's hand. "I need a beer and I'm sure Emily is ready for a two-step."

A dance? Was the woman crazy? However, Emily was intrigued. She'd never heard the name Zebulon before. She liked it but was embarrassed at the way Brittany talked to, and almost manhandled, the tall, handsome cowboy with the low, sexy voice. She swallowed hard. This wasn't going to be an easy evening. Cowboys surrounded her, and she never in her wildest dreams would have thought she'd think someone in tight fitting jeans and a cowboy hat would be handsome, but Zeb was.

His blue eyes locked and held her gaze. She couldn't make herself look away but she managed to take a step back. If he asked her to dance she'd be mortified! "I'm sure if the gentleman wants to leave, we should let him." Why couldn't Brittany just let him go and get it over with?

"Don't be silly. Y'all need to dance."

The man finally broke eye contact and she managed to catch her breath. How could a *cowboy* have that kind of effect on her? Or any man, for that matter? After what she'd been through with her uncle, who was a rodeo cowboy, she'd steered clear of all men, but mostly those who wore boots and hats. It was hard to do in the state of Texas.

She gave her a stern gaze then glanced back to Zeb. "It's okay, really." She heard Brittany's voice.

"One two-step isn't going to hurt."

Zebulon looked like a perfectly built machine. The denim wranglers hugged his thighs, while the flare at the bottom sat atop his boots at just the right length. His western shirt fit snug across his muscular chest. His bright, white smile mesmerized her when he slightly tipped his rough looking straw hat toward her when they were introduced.

Wow, she had to get these thoughts out of her mind. The wine from supper must have played with her head more than she thought. Thankfully, since she and Brittany knew they'd probably have a few drinks with dinner, they'd decided to take a cab instead of driving. "I don't know how to two-step."

She followed while Brittany led Zeb to a table, never letting go of his hand. Emily thought she would see a protest but she didn't. What kind of relationship did those two have? They seemed to know each other pretty well. In the short time she'd known Brittany, her personality said she'd never met a stranger.

"If you don't know how to country dance, Zeb is the perfect man to teach you. He's the best there is." Brittany took a seat and looked at Zeb. "He'll teach you everything you need to know. Right? Right."

Sitting at the table wasn't what she wanted to do. She wanted to *crawl* under it. Instead, she listened while the other two gave their orders, then she ordered a rum and cola. Once the waitress returned with the drinks she felt a little more at ease. At least she had something to do with her hands.

Zeb played with the corner of the napkin his drink sat on. "How do you two know each other?"

Brittany stood and picked up her glass. "Work. Hey, I'll be right back. I see someone I know over there. You two get to know each other."

Before Emily could bat an eye, Brittany was

gone. Now what was she supposed to do? Left alone with a man she didn't know. A cowboy no less, a handsome, sexy cowboy, in a bar at that! Talk about uncomfortable. She would be sure to tell her new, so-called *friend*, what she thought about it. But his deep voice sounded anything but threatening.

"So you girls work together?"

"Yes."

"Do you come here a lot?"

Oh, great, small talk. She didn't want to look at him, but once she did he held her captive. "This is my first time. You?" She studied him for a moment. His dusty colored hair was longer than most cowboys. It hung below his ears and curled loosely beneath his hat in the back. She liked it.

"No, I used to, but...not anymore."

She saw sadness in his eyes and wondered what was behind it. "I see." He took a gulp of beer and she noticed the way his Adam's apple moved in his throat. Heat rushed through her. She smiled back at him when he gave her a knowing grin. If only he wore a Polo shirt and slacks, she might be tempted.

He nodded. "You were dragged here against your will weren't you?"

"Sort of." She took a sip of her drink, sat back in her chair and listened to the band. Just because she didn't necessarily care for cowboys didn't mean she didn't like country music. It was all she listened to.

"You can come clean with me. I've known your friend for a long time and I know how... persuasive she can be."

So Brittany had known this man for a long time. That was interesting. Something in his eyes said she could trust him. She nodded. "She really twisted my arm and I'm okay with it. However, I will know what to expect in the future." She laughed. "I was wondering why the other two ladies that had dinner with us tucked tail and ran after we ate." The handsome man's smile was endearing.

"Yeah, but you can't help but love her. That girl's heart's as big as this state."

It was nice that he'd taken up for the thin, small framed woman that stood a head shorter than she. "Yes, there's a kindness in her eyes. I noticed that right away."

She grew wearier of the circumstances by the minute. Something about this man stirred unfamiliar feelings inside her she didn't understand or didn't want to understand. She glanced about the room. Was Brittany ever coming back? Where was the woman? She scanned the dance floor then the surrounding tables. There was no sign of her.

Her leg brushed Zeb's under the table and sparks flew between them when their eyes met. Butterflies fluttered in her stomach and she felt like a school girl meeting the boy of her dreams for the first time.

"Wanna dance?" He couldn't believe those words had just come out of his mouth. The look of uncertainty crossed Emily's face. "It's okay, really. Brittany was right. I'm a pretty good dancer. I'll show you how." He actually offered to teach someone how to two-step? What had gotten into him?

"No, no, thank you."

"It's not that hard."

"In these heels?"

She pulled her leg from beneath the table. Her skirt was above her knees a few inches and her high-heeled boots went half way up her shapely calf.

He swallowed hard and wondered how it would feel to run his hand up the soft skin of her leg, only to rest—What the hell was he thinking? His mouth moved faster than his brain. "You could take them off." Her smile was tight but still friendly. He knew the answer to that before she moved her leg beneath the table again, with an obvious attempt not to touch his.

"I don't think so."

Her rejection told him all he needed to know. She wasn't interested and he wasn't either. Thoughts of the happiness he'd once known with the woman he loved, then the tragedy of their love falling apart, made him wonder why he was even still at the club. He guessed looking into Emily 'who-ever-she-was', eyes made him momentarily forget the pain he'd felt for so long.

"Sure." He took the last sip of his beer. It was time for him to go.

"Hey, kids, how's it going?"

Zeb stood and looked at Brittany. "Speakin' of goin', I'm doin' just that. I have an early day tomorrow."

"Oh, I was just going to ask you to dance."

He glanced down at the pretty woman who moments ago he sat beside. "Looks like dancin' ain't in the cards for me tonight." He pushed his chair in then said, "Miss Emily, it was nice to meet you."

She offered a handshake. "Nice to meet you, too."

When her hand gripped his in a firm but gentle caress, his body betrayed him once again and reacted to the softness of her skin, her touch. It had been a long time since he'd felt those feelings and logic told him to run. Run for his life, his heart!

Surely Emily's pulse was going to run away with itself. "What were you thinking, Brittany? I don't even know that guy. You left me in a very uncomfortable situation and I didn't like it."

"Gee, Emily, I'm sorry. Zeb's such a nice guy and you're a wonderful woman. I just thought y'all would hit it off."

"I'm not into one night stands."

Brittany laughed. "That man is anything but a one night stand. He's a keeper."

"Well, I'm not looking for a keeper. I'm perfectly happy being—"

"Bored? Living a life of taking homework to keep your nights and weekends occupied? You need a man."

"If he's such a catch, why don't *you* go after him?" Just the thought made her jealous.

"Are you kidding? He's like my brother. Besides, I have my eyes on another cowboy."

The other woman stared wantonly across the room, but *her* thoughts went back to Zebulon. No matter how hard she tried, she couldn't deny there was something about him that intrigued her. However, she knew no relationship between them could happen. She wouldn't allow it. Even though

Brittany said he was a good man, experience taught her no man was above being abusive.

CHAPTER THREE

The door securely locked behind her, Emily wanted a snack. An apple with peanut butter and a small glass of milk sounded good. While she prepared her food, she thought of how pleased she was that Brittany had taken her light reprimand well. Hurting the girl's feelings wasn't what she wanted to do. She just never wanted to be put in that position again.

She made her way into the living room, sat on the couch and reached for the remote. It wasn't in its usual spot. Where could she have put it? She glanced around the living area and noticed the pillows on the sofa were out of place, or at least not positioned the way she usually had them. Then she saw the remote, along with the one to her stereo, neatly placed side by side on the television stand. She never put them there What was going on? This was past strange.

A sudden chill invaded the room and she set her plate on the coffee table. Was she going crazy? First she thought someone had made her bed, now this? She turned every light in the apartment on and went around making sure all the windows were locked, and they were. She went to the entry hall to get her purse and removed her pepper spray from the side pocket. Returning to her snack, she placed the weapon beside her on the couch. It would be under her pillow as well. Tomorrow she would talk to the Meyers and, for safety reasons, see if they would change the locks. She couldn't imagine who would have a key except for a prior tenant.

Remote in hand, she flipped channels until she found an old re-run of *I Love Lucy*. She needed a good laugh. Why couldn't life still be that simple?

Her thoughts drifted back to the man she'd met that night. She realized no one mentioned Zeb's last name. Oh, well, it didn't matter anyway. She'd never see him again and that was okay with her. Or was it?

Taking her plate to the kitchen she wondered, for the umpteenth time, why her father abandoned her and her mother. She was only four when he left. What had she done? Why didn't he love her enough to be in her life? And why had her mother turned to drugs and alcohol? Had she been that bad of a child? She didn't know if she'd ever get answers to these questions. They'd plagued her all of her life.

After her mother's overdose, she'd gone to live with Aunt Ruby and her no good husband, Able Collins. It seemed Ruby was the only person in the world who loved her. It was obvious Abe didn't. Even he blamed *her* for Ruby divorcing him. No matter how much Auntie tried to convince her none of it was her fault, she couldn't let the guilt go. If there ever was a man in her life who had loved her, she might reconsider a relationship, but for now—

Her muscles tensed. What was that noise? She held her breath and listened intently. Was someone walking in the hallway? No, it was closer than that. Or was it? Closing her eyes, she tried to calm her quickened pulse, then she heard a man and woman laughing and a door closed, muffling the sounds.

She needed to get a grip. Knowing her imagination was going to drive her out of her mind until she got her locks changed, she grabbed her mace and headed for bed. Funny, she'd never checked her bedroom door for a lock before, but was compelled to do so then breathed a sigh of relief when she found it.

"I'm sorry to bother you on Saturday, but I have a… well, an issue." Emily liked Mrs. Meyer. The woman was probably in her mid to late fifties and for some reason, reminded her of Auntie. Not because they actually resembled each other, but their warmness, kind eyes and age were somewhat alike.

"You just come on in here, you're no bother."

Emily stepped inside. The landlord's loft wasn't as big and spacious as hers, yet it was decorated warm and homey. Immediately, she felt welcome.

"Does this have something to do with your apartment, Emily? It's okay if I call you Emily, isn't it?"

"Of course, I would prefer it."

"And you can call me Opal."

The warm smile on Opal's face eased her reservations about broaching her dilemma. "Yes, it does have to do with my place."

"Then let me get my husband." Mrs. Meyer closed the door. "Willie?"

"Yes, dear?"

"Miss Tipton is here to speak to us. She has a problem."

Willie Meyer entered the room with a sandwich in one hand and a glass of tea in the other. Emily knew at that moment there was no pretense to these people. They were for real and she trusted them. "Hi, Mr. Meyer, sorry to interrupt your lunch."

"You didn't interrupt anything. I'm still eating aren't I?" He chuckled and took another bite.

His short, round stature said he could probably go without a few meals, but then he wouldn't appear as jolly. "Yes, sir, I guess you are."

He sat in a recliner. "What kind of problem are you having?"

"Have a seat." The older woman patted a place next to her on a loveseat.

"Thank you." She did as requested then said, "Well, this is kind of silly, but I feel like someone may have been in my house while I was gone?" A look of disbelief crossed Willie Meyer's face and now she felt stupid for even thinking it herself.

"Who would do that? We've never had that kind of trouble before. Have we, honey?" Willie sent a questioning glance to his wife.

"Not at all." Opal looked at Emily. "What makes you think that?"

"When I got home from work last evening, it looked as if someone had... well, remade my bed. I made it before I went to work, and it was smooth, but when I got home it was perfect. My aunt Ruby started straightening it for me a few years ago, but she's not here. Then I thought I probably did it unconsciously, but I know I didn't."

Willie took a drink of tea then set the glass on the end table. "That sounds reasonable. So, what is the problem?"

Now she was beginning to wonder if she should just let the whole thing drop. No, she refused to be afraid to be alone in her own apartment. "Last night I went out with a friend. I didn't get home until after midnight and I wanted to watch some T.V. but I couldn't find my remote."

Mrs. Meyer patted Emily's leg with her hand. "My goodness, if I had a dollar for every time my husband lost our remote, I'd be a rich woman."

"Yes, I know that's usually the case, but most of the time I keep in on the end table by the sofa, I'm really not OCD about things being in their proper place. Not only could I not find the remote, which I finally did but not where I had put it, but the pillows on the sofa were out of place." She looked first at Opal, then at Willie. "I'd like to replace the locks if possible. I really don't think anyone is coming in, and there's a logical reason for all of this, but it would make me feel better."

Willie took the last bite of his sandwich and wiped his mouth with a napkin. "Then, replace the locks we'll do. We don't want you to feel unsafe in your own home. Right, Mother?"

"Whatever you say, dear."

Emily could have sworn she heard an underlying tone of irritation in Opal Meyer's voice. Maybe it was because of the extra expense. "I'll be glad to pay for it myself."

Willie stood then picked up his empty tea glass. "Absolutely not. It's our responsibility to keep our tenants happy and that's what we intend to do. I'll get it done this afternoon."

Opal stood and straightened her dress. "I'm sure we have an extra set of locks around here somewhere. We'll get you taken care of, don't you worry about a thing. You have to keep your mind clear so you can keep up with that new job of yours, and we want you to be safe."

She felt bad for thinking the older woman was irritated. She was just as friendly as ever and sounded genuinely concerned. "Thank you." She glanced at the man returning from the kitchen. "And thank you for being so prompt. I'll sleep better tonight, that's for sure."

An hour had passed since she'd gone to the Meyers'. She'd decided to do some laundry while she waited for Willie. A knock sounded at the door. Could he be here already?

She folded the last towel, went to the door and opened it, expecting to see the chubby old fellow, but nobody was there. First she looked one way down the hallway, then the other. Nothing. She heard it again. It wasn't someone knocking at her door at all. It was someone in the loft above hammering a nail or something.

The door clicked shut behind her and she turned the bolt lock. Maybe Brittany was right. She needed to get a life. Apparently, her boredom was making her mind play tricks on her. Walking back to the laundry room, she heard another knocking sound. Was that the door or the neighbor hammering? Tap, tap, tap, again. For sure it was the door.

This time when she opened it, Willie Meyer's smile greeted her. His cheeks flushed and eyes sparkled. If he wasn't bald on top with salt and pepper colored hair on the sides, and if he had a white beard, he might remind a person of Santa Claus. "Hi, come on in." She almost laughed at the loaded down work belt he had strapped around his thick middle. He was so cute!

"Sorry it took me so long."

Was he kidding? "It's only been an hour. I'd say you're pretty prompt." She watched him put a doorknob and a bolt-lock on the 'catch-all' table in the entryway.

"Now, these both use the same key. That way you won't have to mess with two. It's a new set, and no one else, besides you, me, the missus and the maintenance man, will have a key. So, you stop fretting, you hear?"

"Yes, sir." She listened to him grunt and groan while he worked until he finally finished.

"There you go, little lady. No more worries. But if anything else happens, don't hesitate to let us know." He put his tools into the proper places of his belt. "We'll see you later."

"Thank you, Mr. Meyer."

"Call me Willie. We're all family around here."

"Okay, Willie, thanks." A warm feeling filled her heart as she watched the jolly old man waddle down the hall. Why couldn't her aunt have taken up with Willie Meyer in school instead of that creep she married? Did Willie know Able?

She breathed a heavy sigh, closed the door and started back to finish her laundry. She'd never know why things turned out like they did, but she did feel better about being alone in her loft.

Zeb glanced at his light blue, nineteen seventy-two Chevy pickup with a white top. He'd spent many hours restoring that truck to its original condition. The only thing that wasn't original was what was under the hood. He was sure he could take any hotrod in Dallas.

He opened the driver's side door and spoke to his two Labrador retrievers, Buck and Earl, who went almost everywhere with him. "Get in and scoot over, y'all." The dogs' tails slapped against the leather seats as they did what they were told, but not before Buck licked him in the face. "Thanks, bud, but I've already had a shower today."

With his K-9 friend's properly sitting in the passenger seat, he climbed into the truck and cranked it up. Yes, he loved this truck, but he hated his job, especially on a day like today. He decided not to show his client the vulgar video of her husband and the other woman on the dance floor and was glad he did. The photos were enough to give her the answer she needed. Her husband was cheating. He just didn't understand it. She was a beautiful woman and a nice person who didn't deserve the heartbreak.

Sometimes he wished he was back in law enforcement. He missed the excitement of the chase, the call of duty and the respectability of the job. Today he felt like one of those lowlife private investigators in the movies. The kind of creep who had a seedy office filled with smoke and lights so dim you couldn't see a damn thing. Kind of like The Hitchin' Post.

Why did he have to think of that place? It only brought back memories of *her*. He pulled onto the street. Emily had been on his mind off and on since the moment he met her. She'd faded in an out of his dreams and made him toss in his sleep. Thoughts of her long, shapely legs came to mind. "What, are ya' nuts? Stop fantasizing" He glanced over at his dogs. "It's been just us three for a while, now, and I intend to keep it that way. Oh, but I wish y'all could see her. She's somethin' else."

It was inevitable he'd come face to face with her again since he did work for Kail, Cooper and Mills now and again. Bob Mills was a wonderful lawyer, as were the other two, but Mills had been the one to get the settlement for his fiancée's parents after the accident. He'd always be indebted to the man for his time and effort on the case.

Now he remembered why he wasn't a ranger anymore, and the memories reminded him why he would never be again.

CHAPTER FOUR

Why did the phones always ring off the hook in a law office on Monday mornings? Emily was glad she wasn't the one on the switchboard. Poor Brittany's hands were full but she was efficient and had it all under control.

This was a busy firm and she was proud to be part of it. Though she was an employee of the company, she was the personal, legal secretary to Mr. Mills. He was a nice man and she'd felt a bond with him right away. He seemed to care about her, her feelings and ideas. He was a smart man and she found herself wanting to be the same kind of boss.

Maybe one day she could go back to school and fulfill her dream of a law degree, but for now, it had to wait. She couldn't afford the fees and didn't want to have to pay back student loans for the next ten years of her life. Her aunt offered to help, but she didn't feel right taking money from Auntie to pay her tuitions.

Even though Auntie had said she'd gotten a large inheritance from a long lost relative, Emily didn't want to take advantage of it. When she'd asked Ruby who the relative was, the woman acted like she didn't hear, or simply ignored the question. She was afraid to press the issue. Besides, it really wasn't any of her business.

She heard her office door open and glanced up from her computer. "Brittany, come in." She plopped her small frame onto one of the chairs.

"Whew, I finally got a break. I'm sure glad Dad hired that new girl Jordan for me to train."

"Dad?"

"Yeah, my dad's your boss."

She'd worked there two months and knew good and well Brittany was Robert Mills' daughter, but she couldn't resist teasing the young woman. "He is?"

"Yep." The young woman took a peppermint from the container on her desk and popped it into her mouth. "Brittany Mills, that's me."

"Well, who'd a thunk it?!" She joined Brittany in laughter and couldn't believe her resemblance to her father, especially the green eyes. She really liked the girl, and every time she looked at her it made her wonder if she looked like her own father. Was he tall, what color were his eyes? She shook the thought and turned back to Brittany.

"Wow, Emily, you made a joke. Totally unlike you."

"You don't really know me, either, Miss Mills."

"Maybe we should be new best friends and get to know each other better. I haven't had a best pal in a long time."

Emily didn't remember *ever* having a *true* best friend. She conceded to herself Randle was a true friend, but she'd never had a best *girl*-friend. Maybe it would be enjoyable, for a change, to hang out with the girls. "Hmm, that sounds like fun. Pinky swear we'll be besties for life?"

Brittany stood and stuck out the little finger on her right hand. "Pinky swear!"

Somehow, she believed her. She reached across the desk, stuck out her right pinky finger and grasped hold of Brittany's. "BFF's." She felt like a high school girl instead of a grown woman, but then, she'd never had a real childhood where she enjoyed being a kid, so what the hell. Maybe it was time to start living.

"Cool! Hey, I gotta get back to the switchboard. The man of my dreams might decide to call and I won't be there to answer." She walked to the door. "Speaking of that, have you decided to let me give Zeb your number?"

The cowboy was a subject she didn't want to broach. "Why are you so short when you're dad's so tall?"

Brittany squinted. "You're avoiding the question."

She turned back to focus on her computer screen. "So are you."

"My mom's shorter than me. You should see my parents together. Totally unnatural that I could have even been conceived with that height difference."

The giggle escaped before she could stop it. "That's just wrong. You shouldn't even think those things about your mom and dad."

Opening the door, Brittany glanced back at Emily and said, "I answered your question, now answer mine."

She pointed to the doorway. "Not interested, now outta here."

"Okay, okay, just thought I'd try."

The corners of her mouth lifted into a grin when the door clicked shut. She'd thought about cowboy more than once over the weekend. Truth be known, she was interested, but her fears would forever keep her from acting on it.

~ ~ ~

Brittany stepped inside the elevator. "I'm glad this building has an elevator. I don't think we'd ever make it up three flights of stairs to your loft carrying all these bags."

Emily pushed the third-floor button and the sliding doors closed. "You're right. I don't think I've ever bought this much stuff at one time in my life."

"Did you have a good time, though?"

The bell rang indicating they were at their destination and the door slid open. "I had a blast."

"That's all that matters."

Emily was loving life right now. She had never laughed as much as she had at Brittany's folly. Why hadn't she let loose before? Being reserved and proper wasn't always what it was cracked up to be.

Auntie had tried to get her to relax about life, but she couldn't let herself go. Did her dread of being hurt again, not only physically, but mentally, keep her from living all these years? She realized now being focused was her shield.

She set her shopping bags on the floor, got her keys out of her purse, unlocked the door then grabbed her new purchases once again. "Come on, let's put these in my bedroom."

Brittany followed Emily inside. "Wow, this is a really nice place."

"Thank you, I was lucky to get it." She placed the bags on the floor at the foot of the bed as did her friend, and was excited to go through them. First, however, she wanted a root beer. "Hey, you want a soda?"

"No thanks, I'd better be going. I have a hot date tonight."

"Oh? With the man of your dreams?"

"I don't think so, but he's going to buy me a steak, so I don't want to be late."

Emily saw her friend to the door. "You're a hopeless case. Poor guy doesn't even know what he's getting himself into."

"Poor guy? He's getting to spend the evening with me."

She loved her new bestie. She watched Brittany walk down the hall then closed the door and went into the kitchen. After opening the fridge, she grabbed a soda and went to sit on the sofa. She took a couple of gulps then belched out loud and laughed at herself. She'd have never done that before, even though she was alone and nobody would know.

The fluffy pillows on the back of the couch felt soft when she leaned her head against them and thought about her life's changes over the past few months. Her job had been a dream come true. Mr. Mills was a wonderful man and a great boss. He seemed to take a special interest in her. He'd been more than generous in helping her financially. Well, that wasn't all him, the company did most of that, but now she was stable and even had some money in the bank. Money she'd earned.

Brittany and her father were so close. She could tell they loved each other a lot. It made her sad to know that her own father didn't want her. Never loved her and would never even know her. Sometimes she found herself wishing she could change places with her new friend, even if it was only for a day.

Not wanting to have a pity party after such a fun day, she sat up, took the last few drinks of her soda and headed for the bathroom. Her intention was to take a shower, go through her new things and put them away, get into her pajamas then watch a couple of movies she'd wanted to see.

She dropped her clothes carelessly to her bedroom floor, then went to the bathroom, started the shower and stepped inside. The warm water felt wonderful on her skin. She relaxed against the back wall and let the droplets run in sheets down her body.

Somehow, her thoughts drifted to tight jeans, cowboy boots and hat... Zebulon. She'd never taken a shower with a man but wondered what it would be like to be naked with him, while the water caressed them. What his hands would feel like against her breasts rubbing gently with the lather of the soap.

Just the thought of him brought fantasies she'd never had before. Dreams, that's all they were, they'd never be reality, she had to remember that.

~ ~ ~

Thank God Emily's ugly friend finally left. He thought she'd never shut up! No one was as beautiful as his princess Emily, his virgin princess. She wasn't like that whore she'd gone shopping with. They may both have dark hair and green eyes, but the friend looked like a mangy alley cat on the prowl. He'd never allow his precious princess to be like that.

He watched his princess close and lock the front entrance then he enjoyed seeing her relax on the couch with a soda until she did the unthinkable. She belched out loud. It was all he could do to keep his presence unknown. He wanted to lash out at her for doing such a disgusting thing! Taking a slow, deep breath he calmed himself. There would be plenty of time to reprimand her when they were together. For now, he would let it go.

Princess got up and swiftly walked into her bedroom then he heard the bathroom door close. When she turned on the shower he pushed hard on the vent grate and eased himself down, grateful the builder had installed a built-in ceiling to floor bookcase. Since she hadn't filled it with much of anything since she moved in he had the perfect ladder.

This was the first time he'd entered her apartment with her inside. Until now he'd only watched from behind the vent cover, or through the massive expanse of windows across the front of her loft apartment. It was perfect for watching her from the place he rented across the street, and he had easy access to the roof from the outside service ladder attached to the building. He couldn't have done better if he'd chosen it for her.

He hurried into her bedroom and inhaled deeply. Her scent was everywhere and it was so delicious. Funny how she never knew where that first bottle came from, yet she'd loved his choice so well she'd bought it several times since. Now all he had to do was pick out her clothes for today. What had the little vixen bought?

The shopping bags invited him to explore her purchases, and for the most part he liked her choices, all except the shorts. She looked fantastic in shorts and he loved her legs, but it wasn't right for other men to look at them. He pulled out a red and pink printed sundress of modest length and cut. Yes, this was it!

Now for her undergarments. He saw several bags from his favorite lingerie store and opened them. Perfect, a new lace bra in pink, and matching panties. He wished he could watch her dress, better yet, he wished he could dress her himself. There was nothing like stretching the elastic around a shapely body, pushing her perfect breasts into place in the lace bra cups then fastening those tiny hooks. She should probably have help so her cleavage could puff out the way he liked. Hell, all men liked puffy cleavage but this one was for his eyes only.

Once his choices were made he laid the dress on the bed as if she had it on. He put the panties on top of the dress where they should be located underneath, and did the same with the bra, making sure there were no wrinkles in the fabric and everything was straight. There, good. No, excellent! She would look fantastic and he couldn't wait to—

The shower stopped and that was his immediate cue to leave, but he had to pick up the pile of dirty clothes she'd left at the foot of the bed. She knew better than to be sloppy. He lifted the lid of her rattan hamper and tossed them in but pulled out her panties. He shoved the garment into his pocket so he could saver the smell of them later. He took a last glance around the room. Better. No messes— ever! He'd teach her what she needed to know, but in the meantime, he'd keep picking up after her because she was so beautiful and he couldn't help himself. The complete perfect package was still a work in progress, but he had time—lots of time.

~ ~ ~

Once Emily was through washing, she stepped out of the shower, grabbed a towel, wrapped it around her head then got another so she could dry off. She was excited to try on her new outfits so she hurriedly dried her hair then opened the door leading to her room. Which one would she try first?

Panic took her breath and her legs threatened to collapse beneath her. "No!" She glanced around the room for the intruder, no one was there. She had to think fast. Quickly she ran to the bedroom door, closed and locked it then grabbed her cell phone from her dresser. She wished she had her mace but it was in her purse. Her purse! Had she been robbed, too? "Who could have done this?"

Her heart pounded and she fought down the bile in her throat. Someone had been in her room while she was in the shower. The clothes she'd taken off and left on the floor only a short while ago were gone. They were gone!

She glanced at her bed and thought her heart would stop altogether. Her blood ran through her veins like an icy mountain stream. Laid out perfectly on her bedspread was one of the new bras she bought that day and a pair of matching panties. The undergarments rested on top of the new sundress she'd purchased, as if someone handpicked the outfit for her.

Why? Why was someone doing this to her? Vulnerability invaded every cell in her body and she realized she was near naked. She had to get some clothes on and call Brittany. She couldn't stay here alone another minute.

Once she was dressed, she went into the bathroom, closed and locked the door to make her call. At least if someone was still in the apartment they'd have to get through two barriers to get to her.

Her hand trembled while she pushed the address book button on her phone. It was impossible to stay calm when someone might be lurking outside her bedroom door. She shuddered and was so scared she thought she was going to be sick. Closing her eyes she inhaled a deep breath and whispered, "Calm down."

Tremors rushed through her as she placed the phone to her ear. When she heard Brittany's voice her fear surfaced, then the tears came.

CHAPTER FIVE

Sunday afternoon and Emily once again found herself in the loft alone, but only for a short while. Brittany had gone home to get her work clothes for Monday morning, then was coming back to spend the night.

Unable to make herself go into her bedroom until Brittany returned, she decided to take the opportunity to call Randle and ask his advice. He was always level headed about these things. She picked up the phone, dialed his number and waited for him to answer.

"Well, hi, Miss Tipton. How's Dallas treating you? You liking it?"

It was good to hear his voice. He had a way of calming her. "Hey, Randle, I love it." She heard the hesitation in her own voice. "It's treating me okay. How are you?"

"I'm good." He drew out the word. "But something's wrong on your end. What *aren't* you telling me?"

She chuckled. "How do you know something's bothering me?"

"I can hear it in your voice. What's going on? You okay?"

"You know me too well, my friend. Randle..." Could she bring herself to tell him? It made her tremble just thinking about it, much less saying it out loud.

"Come on, Emily, spit it out."

The genuine concern in his voice spurred her on. Coming right out with it was the fastest way to get it over with. "I think someone's getting into my house and doing things."

"Getting into your house? Emily, that's scary. Doing things? Like what?"

She went on to tell him of the weird happenings. His reaction made her realize she'd made the right decision about not being alone in the loft.

"Sweetie, you've got to get the authorities involved in this. You might be in real danger."

"I'm not going to be alone tonight. My friend Brittany is staying with me."

"That's all well and good, but maybe you should call your aunt Ruby to come spend some time with you."

Why hadn't she thought of that? "Awesome idea. I knew you'd know what to do. I'll call her."

"Promise?"

"I promise."

"*And* the police. You've got to let them know

what's happening. You hear me?"

"I hear you." She didn't want to involve the police just yet. Surely it wasn't anything that serious.

"Okay, then. Please keep me updated."

"I will. Thanks for listening."

"I'm here for you if you need to talk. I'd come to Dallas myself but now's not a good time. Give me a couple of weeks, and if you need –"

"Randle, I understand, you're a married man. You can't be at my side at my beck and call. Don't fret. I'm going to call Aunt Ruby as soon as we get off the phone."

"Thanks for understanding. That doesn't mean I love you any less."

"I know. Love you, too. Bye, Randle."

"Bye, bye."

She pushed the red 'end' button and realized how lucky she was to have him as a friend. If she *really* needed him, he'd be there in a flash. She only hoped his wife would understand. Now, she needed to call her aunt.

She went to her contacts and speed dialed Ruby. The phone rang once, twice, then on the third ring she heard her aunt's familiar voice.

"Hello."

"Hi, Aunt Ruby, how are you?" She'd only spoken to the woman a few times since she'd moved to Dallas and she missed her more than she thought.

"I'm good, honey, but I was just about to walk out the door to catch my flight."

"Flight? Where are you going?" Maybe she was

coming to visit her. Perfect timing.

"Don't you remember? I have a trip planned. I'm taking that Caribbean tour cruise I've dreamed about forever. My plane leaves for Seattle in two hours, so I need to get to the airport."

Her heart sank to the pit of her stomach. How could she have forgotten? Ruby had planned it for over a year. "Oh, yes! I bet you're excited." She refused to tell her aunt what was going on. Why should she ruin this special time in this woman's life when she'd given up so much of it for her?

"Oh, you can't imagine! My heart skips a beat just thinking about it. I've never been on the ocean before. How are you, honey, are you okay?"

"F-fine, I'm just fine. I won't keep you. Go and have a wonderful time. See if you can find you a sweet man like Mr. Meyer and bring him home with you." Her aunt's laughter rang through the phone.

"It's a thought!"

She knew a man was the last thing on Ruby Collins's mind. "I love you, Auntie. Maybe you can come see me when you get back."

"I love you, too, and I think that's a wonderful idea. Take care now."

Tears welled in her eyes. "I will. Bye-bye." The click from the other end of the phone said Ruby had hung up. A reminder she was alone in this place.

What was she going to do now? She couldn't ask Brittany to sleep on the couch for the rest of her life. If her friend didn't still live at home, she'd consider staying with her, but she wouldn't impose on her boss and his family.

The doorbell rang and she jumped at the sudden

shatter of silence. "Damn! I've got to get a grip." As she went toward the door, she heard Brittany from the other side.

"It's me."

When she opened the door, she was never so happy to see another person in her life. "Hey, glad you're back." The other woman walked past her carrying an overnight case and a paper bag. "What's in the sack?"

"Popcorn, a bottle of wine and a movie. I figure if we're going to chill, we should do something constructive."

"You call drinking wine and sitting in front of the television constructive? I think you're confused, Brittany."

"Nope, nothing better to soothe the nerves than relaxation."

She had to admit, it sounded like a good idea. "Alrighty, then, I'll get the corkscrew."

The salt of the popcorn, along with the taste of the wine, hit the spot. Emily was glad the movie was a comedy. Drama was the last thing she needed more of. However, she had to figure out what she was going to do. "Hey, I called my aunt, but she's going on a cruise and can't come visit. I think I'll just get one of those chain locks and when I'm home, use it."

"Emily, that doesn't make any sense. You need to figure out who keeps getting in here. It's not safe for you to be here at all. At least not alone. I talked to my dad and—"

"I'm not going to impose on your family." The look on Brittany's face almost made her laugh.

"If you'd let me finish…"

"Sorry." She took another bite of popcorn then paused the movie.

"I talked to my dad and he has some ideas. He's going to run them by you tomorrow at work. He's very concerned. Almost as worried about you as he would be if it were me in the same situation. He really likes you. I can tell."

She'd felt a strong bond with Bob Mills since the first day she'd met him. "I really like him, too. I wish my dad could have been like yours."

"Yeah, he's a pretty good pop, that's for sure. Anyway, stop worrying, he'll take care of it. What does your dad do?"

Never having talked about her life to anyone before, she wasn't sure she was ready now, but Brittany seemed genuinely interested. "I don't know. I don't even know who he was or if he's dead or alive. He ran away when I was four and left me and my mother."

"Why?"

"My mom said it was because of me. He never wanted children, then I had to come along." She blinked back tears that welled in her eyes. That was the first time she'd ever said those words out loud.

"That's terrible. I can't imagine why a mother would say that to her child even if it were true!"

"She wasn't in her right mind. My mom turned to drugs and alcohol soon after he left. She overdosed a year later and that's when I went to live with my aunt."

"You poor thing. Did your aunt try to find your dad or anything?"

She took a sip of wine and sat quietly for a moment. "She said she did, but I'm not really sure." Brittany looked as if she had a revelation and Emily knew she was about to hear it.

"Hey, with all the internet stuff nowadays, why don't we try to find him. We at least know his last name's Tipton, that's a start."

"Won't work." She'd had the same idea after she turned eighteen and could make her own decisions, but at that time, she thought if he didn't want to know her, to hell with him.

"Why? We can start with the town you were born in."

"His name's not Tipton. I don't know what it is, or was. Tipton was my mom's maiden name and she legally had my name changed to that after he left. She made my aunt swear and sign legal papers that she would never tell me who he was."

"What? How awful. Looks like your aunt would have given in after you were grown."

"I don't blame her. She's a woman of her word and I respect her for that. She's been very good to me. Even before she divorced her husband, she protected me from his wrath."

"He sounds like a creep."

"Oh, trust me, creep is a nice name to call Able Collins." Able was the reason she feared cowboys. She knew it was stupid, just because someone was a cowboy didn't mean they were like her uncle, but still, it was a childhood fear she couldn't get past. She'd had enough of talking about her sordid childhood. What happened to finally make her aunt get a divorce was something she didn't want to relive. "You know what? We need to finish this movie and get some sleep. Morning will come before we know it." She hit the play button, then immediately hit pause.

Brittany sat up straight. "Did you hear that?"

Emily swallowed hard at the sound that came from... somewhere. "I did, but it's probably just the creaking of this old building." She tried to calm herself as much as she was trying to calm Brittany.

"Are you sure? That sounded like a definite thump. Does someone live above you?"

"Yes, but it didn't sound like it came from there. I don't hear things from that apartment much. I can't tell where it came from." This loft was someplace she loved living, but if this kept up, she might have to move. "Don't worry, really, this place creaks and thumps all the time." It was hard for her to stay calm, but she had to. Where else could they go at this point? "Want to finish the movie or go to bed?"

"I don't think I could sleep right now. Let's watch it."

Emily hit play once again and thought about the noise. Goose flesh rose on her arms. Was someone watching them? No, that was impossible. Why was this happening?

CHAPTER SIX

Emily moved her mouse over a link and clicked. She enjoyed searching through court files on her computer for the firm. Her company phone buzzed then she heard Mr. Mills' voice over her personal intercom.

"Miss Tipton, would you come in here, please?"

"Yes, sir." She picked up her pad and pencil. Shorthand had become obsolete, but she learned it anyway. It made life much simpler when taking dictation. Upon entering his private office, the look on his face was one of concern. She doubted this was going to be about writing a letter.

Bob Mills gestured to a chair in front of his desk. "Have a seat. I'd like to talk to you."

She put the pencil behind her ear and placed the pad in her lap as she sat down. This conversation would lead to what he had in mind about her problem, but she couldn't figure out why this man was so concerned about her. He barely knew her.

"My daughter informed me of the happenings around your place."

"Yes, sir, she told me."

"What are your thoughts on what to do?"

She had no idea of what to do besides move, or put a padlock on the outside of her door when she left the apartment, then chain lock it when she came home. "I'm not sure. Maybe just make the door more secure." The slightly graying hair over his temples, and his good looks made him even more distinguished, and she had much respect for the man.

Mr. Mills shook his head. "That won't do."

He picked up his phone and dialed zero. Emily knew that would reach Brittany on the switchboard.

"Brittany, would you tell Mr. Cooper to come in here, please." He paused. "Thank you."

"Mr. Cooper?"

"Yes, he's going to help us in this matter."

She wondered what Senior Partner David Cooper could do for her, but whatever it was, she was sure it would be in her best interest. The knock sounded at the door and she stood out of respect to the other senior partner of the firm.

"Come in."

The door opened and the sight of the cowboy hat caused her to drop her note pad. Damn, was she ever going to get over her fear? Her heartbeat slowed when she recognized the tall man who wore the cowboy hat, jeans and the most wonderfully fitting shirt. It was Zebulon. There were those butterflies flitting in her stomach again when he tipped his hat to her. Not flutters of fear, but one she... enjoyed? Now she knew she was losing her mind.

"Miss Tipton."

All she could do was nod her hello. She bent to retrieve her pad then took her seat before her knees buckled beneath her. What was he doing there, in all-of-his cowboy... ness? He took off his straw hat and ran his hands through his tasseled sun-kissed hair. She would like to run her fingers through it the same way. How could she think such a thing? Cowboy hat... hence cowboy... was she crazy?

"Hey, Bob, how ya doin'?" He reached to shake Mills' hand.

"Have a seat, Zeb. I want to talk to you and Miss Tipton about something.

What was going on here? "Excuse me, Mr. Mills, but I thought you said Mr. Cooper was going to help us."

"This *is* Mr. Cooper."

She had to force her gaping mouth shut. Zeb's last name was Cooper? Why hadn't Brittany told her?

"Oh, I'm sorry, I forgot you two haven't met." Bob gestured with his hand. "Zebulon Cooper, this is Emily Tipton."

The moment she grasped the man's hand in a shake, she regretted it. Sensations of pleasure shot up her arm and to her most private parts. Feelings she'd never experienced. Especially by merely shaking someone's hand, well, except in her dreams the last couple of weeks since she'd met him the first time. Dismissing the thought, she remembered her manners. "Mr. Cooper."

The clear blueness of his eyes was overwhelming outside the dim light of the tavern. He shot her a mischievous smile and she thought she'd swoon. Was he ever going to let go of her hand? For that matter, why didn't she release his?

"Good to see you again, Emily."

"Oh, so you *do* know each other?"

"Emily and I met last Saturday. Brittany introduced us."

Never had she liked her name before, but she loved the way it rolled off of Zebulon's tongue. She realized what he'd just told Mr. Mills. Before her boss could ask any more questions she butted in. "Ummm, yes, she did. It's good to see you again, too, Mr. Cooper."

She didn't want Bob to know she went to a bar, though she doubted it would alter his opinion of her. Changing the subject seemed the best way out. If she could keep her breathing steady, she was going to try to meet Zebulon's gaze directly. It was a matter of being able to take those blue eyes and handsome face without being tempted to touch his rugged cheek. "If your last name is Cooper, does that mean you're kin to *our* Mr. Cooper?" His smile was kind this time.

"Sure does. He's my father."

That explained why he and Brittany knew each other so well. They must have grown up together. "I see." She turned her attention back to the man behind the desk. "What's this all about, Mr. Mills?"

Zebulon watched her questioning green eyes dart from him to Mills then back to him. It was obvious she didn't know his father was a senior partner in this firm. Damn she had beautiful lips and her eyes were the color of emeralds in the light of the room. He looked at the man who was like an uncle to him.

He took a seat next to Emily and could almost feel her body heat. Or was it his imagination because he wanted to feel it. The simple handshake between them stirred him. Why did she affect him that way? Now wasn't the time, Mills called him here for a reason. "You said you needed my services, Bob, what's happenin'?"

"It appears Miss Tipton has someone stalking her."

He glanced her way and her gaze was riveted on the other man, the look of disbelief on her pretty face. "A stalker."

"Oh, Mr. Mills, I wouldn't go as far to say I'm being stalked."

"Really, Emily? Then what *would* you call it?"

"Well, I-um... I..."

The uneasiness in her voice said she was unsure and frightened. "Talk to us." Zeb put a finger on her chin, turned her to face him and softened his voice. "Tell me, please." Why did he care so much for someone he'd just met?

She took his hand away and again looked at Bob. "What does all of this have to do with him?"

Now she was talking about him like he wasn't in the room. Hadn't Mills told her why he was there? No, he expected not, since she didn't even *know* who he was. Bob's voice drew his attention.

"I'm going to hire him."

"For what?"

"Zebulon's the best private investigator in Dallas. He'll find out who's doing this to you."

Her eyes focused on him again. Was that fear or distrust he saw in them? Dislike? At that moment, he couldn't read what was behind the look. Then again, why should she trust him, she didn't even know him. "I'll do the best job I can, Emily." He watched her grip the arms of the chair she sat in. Her grasp tightened, turning her knuckles white.

"Private investigator?"

"Yes, that's my job." He didn't understand why she appeared so panicked.

"Sir." She looked at Bob. "Do you really think it needs to go that far? Why can't I just change the locks and get more security on my door?"

Zeb almost smiled at the scolding look the older man shot her. It was one he'd seen many times over the years when the man didn't like the tone Brittany used with him.

"You've already done that once."

"Yes, but—"

Bob Mills cleared his throat. "Any time someone enters your house while you're home, goes into your bedroom when you're only feet away taking a shower, and tampers with your things, it's a dangerous situation." The man looked at Zebulon. "Wouldn't you agree?"

"That happened?" There was no more humor in the situation. This was serious. He sent Emily a questioning glance. Silence was her only answer, but that's all it took for him to know. "When?" He was glad Bob stayed quiet, forcing her to answer. "Emily, when?" She wouldn't look at him but when she spoke her voice betrayed her brave facade.

CHAPTER SEVEN

She'd be damned if she'd let him see fear in her eyes. "Saturday evening." When the cowboy sitting next to her leaned forward to place his hat on Bob Mills' desk, he moved with the grace of a tiger. He'd gotten a serious look in his eye and she knew there would be no dissuading him or her boss.

"Tell me about it. I want to know everything."

Her breath caught in her throat when he turned his chair toward her, sat back and crossed his legs. The game was on and he was supposed to be on her team. What was she going to do? Just being close to him charged her emotions in more ways than one.

Why couldn't she stop the stupid notion to link all cowboys into one category just because her uncle Able was a total ass to her and Auntie? Something deep inside her fought it all the time, but it was failure to conquer the fear that always made her lose the battle.

She took a deep breath then exhaled. No one knew about *all* the times she had suspicions someone had entered her apartment. Not even the Meyer's. She glanced at Mr. Mills then at Zebulon. They both looked genuinely concerned. Maybe it was time to be honest and tell them everything.

Mr. Mills leaned forward and folded his hands on top of his desk. "Emily?"

She blinked back tears thinking this man had been the only one in her life who'd ever acted like he cared. "Yes, sir, I'll tell you two everything."

He sat back once again. "Good, we're listening."

"Soon after I moved into the apartment, I thought I heard someone trying to turn the doorknob." Zebulon's eyes searched her face when she spoke. What was he looking for? Signs she might be lying? Or was it a look of worry?

"How soon after?"

"I'd say about three weeks."

"What did you do?"

"Nothing, really. I heard footsteps moving away from my door and I figured someone was at the wrong loft or something. I did get up to make sure both locks were secured, then went back to the work I'd taken home."

"What came next?"

Man, the cowboy detective was short and to the point. She wondered why Bob was letting him ask all of the questions. She looked once again into the man's mesmerizing eyes. They were the color of the sky at its deepest blue, and his suntanned skin only made their hue richer. She'd never seen a more beautiful color.

"A week or so after that, I felt as if someone was watching me, then I thought I saw someone following me."

Zebulon frowned. "In a car or on foot?"

"After I got out of my car one evening, and started into my apartment, I got a paranoid feeling someone was looking at me. Then I heard some noise come from the shadows. I had a couple of grocery bags in my arms, but I was prepared to drop them and run, then when a cat ran across the parking lot, I figured that was it. The cat was watching me and—"

"It could have been a cat watching, but it could have been a human watching as well, and they might have startled the cat from its hiding place."

She'd never thought of that scenario. Why? She wasn't stupid. Maybe she was just in denial of what was happening. Could she be in real danger? Zeb leaned forward and she smelled the slight fragrance of spice. A shiver ran down her spine. Was it the scent of this man, or the thought she could be in real danger, that caused her apprehension?

"You should have told someone."

"You're right. I realize that now." Zeb took a small, pocket spiral notebook out, flipped it open and began to take notes. The tops of his hands were smooth, and the veins made a perfect pattern on each one, his nails were neatly clipped, but still, they showed signs of hard work. She wondered what their slight roughness would feel like on her bare skin.

She almost chuckled. Now, at twenty-four, she was having thoughts she'd never had before? In a meeting with her boss and a cowboy discussing her life might be in danger? She was losing it.

"Anything else?"

Zebulon could see the wheels in Emily's head turn while she tried to think of anything else. She'd been looking at him curiously, studying him in a way. He assumed she was beginning to trust him. Maybe *hoped* was a better word. Surely, if she trusted Bob Mills' judgment, she'd know he was looking out for her best interest. He put pen to paper when he heard her voice.

"Yes, there were three other times. The first was a week ago Friday when I got home from work. It looked like someone had been sitting on my bed. Later that night Brittany and I went to the... out." She met Zebulon's gaze.

That was a night he'd never forget. He hadn't been able to get her off his mind since. No matter how much he vowed he'd never love again, now fate was trying to test him. He looked back to his notepad when she continued.

"After Brittany dropped me off, I went inside, grabbed a snack and went in the living area to watch some T.V. but I couldn't find my remote. I always keep it in the same place."

Bob smiled. "Wish I could say that about myself. I can never find it when I want it."

Zeb was the same way. The remote control seemed to elude him a lot of the time. "You can get remotes with an auto-finder on it. You know, like the pager button on a portable phone. Then if you lose it, you can go to where the bass is stationed, push the button and your remote will beep." He saw a sweet smile lift the corners of Emily's beautiful mouth.

"Hey," Bob said, "I need to get one of those."

They all laughed and he knew the tension had been broken, if only for a moment. He wondered why someone might be doing this to Emily. She was a virtual stranger to Dallas, so it probably wasn't someone she knew. He studied the woman sitting by him. She was so lovely. For someone with a sordid mind, that could be all it would take to set them in motion. But getting inside her house?

"I'd be the second to get one, Bob," he said. Silence momentarily filled the room. He wanted Emily to continue her accounts in her own time.

She shifted in her chair and her smile faded. "Not only was the remote missing, but the pillows on the sofa were out of place. I'd never leave them like that. Immediately I turned on all the lights, checked the locks on the windows and doors, although being on the third floor, I don't think anyone would try to come in the windows."

Bob nodded. "But as a safety precaution, you did the right thing."

"The next morning I went to my landlords, told them what happened, the locks were promptly changed on my door. Assuring me no one but me, the maintenance man and the Meyers had a key."

There were his first two contacts. "Do you know the maintenance man's name?"

"Dewey something."

"Have you ever had any encounters with him?"

"Not really. I've only spoken to him a couple of times. He's kind of creepy looking, but seems like a nice enough guy."

"Did he come and change the locks?"

"No, I guess he's off on weekends because Mr. Meyer came to change them."

"Really?" He saw admiration in her eyes when she spoke of the owner of the building.

"Mr. Meyer is a sweet old fellow. My aunt knows him from high school. They've kept in touch over the years through class reunions and such. He's a jolly man, and his wife is a sweetheart." She met his gaze. "Both of them have been very good to me."

He made a note to still check with them, look into their past, see what they knew about the maintenance man or if they'd seen anything out of the ordinary. "Did everything stop then?"

She nodded. "Yes, until this Saturday."

"You mean night before last?"

"Yes. That's when I called Brittany to come over."

What could have happened to make her take that precaution? "Tell me about it." Discomfort was evident on her face. He noticed she started twisting her hands together. Moments passed. "Emily? What happened that you felt the need to do that?"

After she told him someone had been in her apartment while she was in the shower, and what they'd done, his heart sank into the pit of his stomach. She was in danger and he was bound and determined to protect her. He started to feel alive again and it was because of this woman. Feelings he thought he'd buried forever were starting to surface again.

He'd lost the only woman he thought he'd ever be in love with and who was special in his life. He didn't know if a relationship between him and Emily would play out in the future, but even if he hadn't been hired to keep her safe, he wouldn't have taken the chance of something happening to her.

The words came out of his mouth before he thought about what he was saying. "You are coming to the ranch with me for a while. I have an extra bedroom."

CHAPTER EIGHT

What did he say? Emily just looked at him, surely he couldn't be serious. Memories of the ranch her aunt and uncle owned when she'd gone to live with them as a child still haunted her. The things that happened there before Aunt Ruby divorced Able were the very things she still feared. She couldn't! "I beg your pardon?" He cleared his throat and she saw determination in his eyes.

"Only temporarily. I have a small, but nice, ranch just outside of town. There's an extra bedroom upstairs with a private sitting room and bathroom. I live downstairs. It'll be fine."

Fine? He thought it would be fine for her to just pack up her things and move to a ranch with a stranger? "I don't think so. I'll get a hotel room if I need to, but thank you for the offer."

"Now, Emily I think Zeb's right you—"

"Mr. Mills! How could you suggest I stay with a strange man?" How could he seriously think she would do that?

"Why, he's not a stranger, I've known this man all his life... and would trust him with mine."

"That may be true, sir, but I've just met him and have no intention of staying at his ranch. He probably has horses, too. I'll get a room, just like I said." She stood and turned toward Zebulon Cooper and he raised to his full height. He towered over her and his shoulders were broad and strong. If anyone could protect her, it was him. She had faith in that. However, she'd be damned if she'd be bullied into doing what this cowboy told her to do. She was in control of her own life and that was that. "Thank you for your offer, Mr. Cooper." Swirling around, she started for the door, but she felt the warmth of Zebulon's hand on her elbow as he gently grasped it.

"Wait. Please."

There was a persuasiveness in his voice she couldn't resist. She closed her eyes and let out a breath. "What is it, Mr. Cooper." He tugged at her arm trying to turn her to face him. If she looked into those eyes of his, she might melt.

"Please, Emily."

The softness in his voice did something to her insides and was most convincing. Her pulse quivered and the warmth of his hand on her elbow spread throughout her body as he held steady, but didn't try to force her to turn.

"Please."

The third time was the charm. Her heart, her body, her soul couldn't resist the earnest sound of his concern. When she turned toward him, the subtle tension of his grasp subsided and he dropped his hand. Their gazes met and she peered into his eyes. It was as if all the air was sucked out of the room. They weren't alone, yet the area seemed to close in, creating a cocoon around them. Their own space, their own time. Maybe staying with him wouldn't be so bad. He stepped toward her and put his hands on her shoulders. Would she ever breathe again?

"Listen to me."

She listened. There wasn't anything else she could do. Why was she reacting like this? Was she going to melt into his arms? If she opened her mouth to say anything would she kiss his inviting lips?

No... no, she had to break this spell. It wouldn't work, it couldn't! She slowly backed out of his grasp and forced herself to put some space between them. "I'm listening."

What had just happened? Zeb had never felt such riveting emotions in his life. Time stood still, if only for an instant. This woman did things to him. He should keep his distance so he wouldn't be in danger of losing his heart. He thought she felt it too, but the coldness in her eyes when she backed away from him said all he needed to know. But her safety was at stake and he'd been hired to do a job.

"You are in danger. Let that sink in for a minute." He moved away from her so the warmth of her body would stop playing tricks with his desire. "Someone has access to your home, they've been inside more than once. They've been there when you were the most vulnerable.

"Your home is where you're supposed to be the safest. But, Miss Tipton, at this time you're not. You have no protection there. You're alone. And you won't be safe in a motel somewhere. That would be an even easier place of access."

He watched as she jumped with the ring of Mills' desk phone. Maybe he was getting through to her.

Bob picked up the receiver. "This is Bob Mills... mmhmm... Yes, she told us. Sure, come on in." He replaced the phone.

The door opened and Brittany walked through the doorway. Emily looked at her and immediately her beautiful face changed. Tears welled in her eyes and she embraced her friend. Zeb wished she had tried to find comfort in his arms, but he was glad there was someone there to soothe her. Then her words told him she now understood the intensity of the situation.

"Oh, Brittany, I've been so foolish."

"Shoot, girl, we all make mistakes. That's why I told Daddy about what was going on with you. You were scared, but I didn't think you were really accepting it's as bad as it is."

"You're right, now I don't know what to do."

He stepped toward the two women. "Brittany, I suggested she come out to the ranch and stay with me until we get this all figured out."

Brittany pushed her back to arm's length.

"That's a *great* idea. You'll love it out there. It's beautiful. Peaceful, quiet but most of all, you'll be safe."

The look on Emily's face was one of disbelief. Why was she fighting it so much? Zeb knew she thought he was a stranger, but she knew these two people and surely had enough faith in them to know they wouldn't steer her wrong.

"You think I should go stay on a ranch?"

Brittany laughed. "Sure. He has the perfect little suite upstairs. It's cozy."

He stepped toward the ladies but focused his attention on Emily. "I have two labs. One chocolate male named Buck and the other one's a yellow female called Earl." The grin that tugged at the corners of her mouth made him smile.

"Earl? What kind of name is that for a dog? A girl dog no less. Poor thing."

He threw his head back in laughter then gave her a mock frown. "Hey, that was my grandma's name. Don't make fun."

"You had a grandma named Earl? Please." She grabbed a tissue from the desk and wiped her nose.

"It's short for Earlene, thank you. I'm sure she'd love to have another female around the house. She and Buck will alert us if anyone is coming. If I'm not there, one can stay in the house with you, the other outside. It will give you double notice. Plus, my foreman will be on the property, too." She bit her lip as if she wanted to ask him something but wasn't sure if she wanted to. What was going through her mind?

"Do you have horses?"

He realized Brittany being there was making her relax and at least discuss things. "Sure, I have six. I'll introduce you to them."

"No, no thank you."

There was no hesitation in her response. The way she shook her head and the look of dread in her eyes was a key to her answer. She damn sure didn't like horses.

Bob stood then looked at Emily. "So, what's your answer? Will you stay with Zebulon for a while? Until we get this all figured out? I'll give you the time off."

Time off? She couldn't afford that. And did she have to make a decision now? "I can't take time off, sir, I can't afford that. Can I give you my answer in the morning?"

"And stay in that loft another night by yourself? Absolutely not, young lady."

Why was he treating her like a child? Maybe it was because she was acting like one. It would be best if she went to stay somewhere else. But to stay with a cowboy on a ranch... with horses?

Brittany looked at her father. "Dang, Dad, lighten up. You'd think you were talking to me or something."

Emily grew to like the younger woman more and more every day. As she looked at father and daughter now, she saw how much they favored each other. Once again she wondered if she looked like her own father.

"And," Mr. Mills said, "don't worry about the time off. You will still make your salary, no matter how long it takes."

She couldn't believe her ears. "I can't ask you to do that. There's no reason I can't come into work."

Brittany turned to Emily. "Are you crazy? I wish he'd make me that offer." She stepped forward. "Emily, come on, you know you should go out there tonight. I'll go with you and help you get your things together then you can follow me out to Zeb's. Okay?"

"Okay?" Zebulon asked.

Mr. Mills peered over at her with raised eyebrows. "Okay?"

It looked as if she had no choice. "Humph. This is a conspiracy." She turned toward the door. "I'll get my purse."

CHAPTER NINE

Emily put her Bluetooth in her ear and dialed Randle's number before putting her car in gear to follow Brittany to the ranch. She wanted to keep him updated on what was happening. When he answered, as always, she was glad to hear his voice.

"Hello."

"Hi, it's me."

"Me? Me could be a number of people. Thank goodness I have caller ID so I know who me is."

"You're such a goofball."

"That's what my wife tells me. What's up? Did you go to the authorities with your suspicions?"

"No, not exactly."

"Emily –"

"I know." She noted the scold in his voice. "I didn't go to the police, but Brittany told her dad what is going on and now I'm going to stay on a ranch with a private investigator who's looking into the happenings."

"A ranch?"

"I know, can you believe it?"

"Not after what you went through with that butthead of an uncle of yours. This must be more serious than you're letting on for you to face your fears like that. I'm proud of you. Is this a lady investigator?"

"No, his name is Zeb Cooper. His father's one of the partners of the firm."

"I'm not crazy about this idea. How well do you know this guy? Is he married, single? Damn, I wish I could be there. Did you call Aunt Ruby?"

"What is this? Twenty questions?"

He chuckled. "I did rattle some off didn't I?" He paused then asked, "Well?"

She cleared her throat. She wasn't crazy about the idea either, but for now she guessed it was the best move. "I don't know him well, but everyone at the firm trusts him. He's not married. I wish you could be here, too, and yes I called Aunt Ruby. She's on a cruise and won't be back for a few more days." She thought about the clothes laying on her bed. "Whoever this is, he's creeping me out."

"Has something else happened?"

"No, not really. A few bangs coming from upstairs, but nothing as drastic as someone laying out my clothes for me." She took a calming breath. "Don't worry, as soon as all this is over, I'll be fine."

"Please don't take any chances. It could mean

the difference between life and death."

When he put it that way she cringed and tried to keep herself together. "Randle, it's not that serious." Was she trying to convince him or herself?

"I hope you're right. You have my number. Call any time. Please?"

"I will, and feel free to call when you can." She went on to tell him where the ranch was located and all the information she knew at that point then hung up.

Her heart raced with anticipation. What was she getting herself into? Spending time on a ranch with a cowboy, horses and dogs? She'd lost her mind! She had to admit the drive was beautiful. It seemed like it took them no time to get out of town and reach their destination.

She saw Brittany's blinker go on and she careened her neck to the right to study the land. A white railed fence lined the dirt lane that led to a white two-story house with blue shutters. Turning onto the narrow road she noted a large barn, a corral, and...an outhouse? He said she'd have her own bathroom. Surely not. The closer she got, she realized it wasn't an outhouse but a building built to look like one, and a well-used one at that.

So the cowboy had a sense of humor. That was just one more thing she'd have to put herself on alert about. Hopefully, he would work fast and find out who was doing this. Then she could get away from him. Although her head told her she could trust him, her heart cried beware.

She braked behind Brittany as the younger woman pulled her car to a stop. Two Labradors, barking at first, ran out to greet them. Once they saw Brittany, they calmed down and continued to approach with tongue's lolling and tails wagging, one brown one blonde. "Buck and Earl," she whispered to herself and wondered which one was which.

Grinning she stepped out of her car. A dog was something she hadn't been allowed to have after Auntie divorced Able. Her aunt Ruby loved cats, so that's what she grew up with, and it was okay with her.

The yard surrounding the house was defined by a white picket fence and was full of thick green grass lined by flower beds, all rich with color. Something she'd always thought she'd like was gardening, but she'd never gotten to do it. It was hard to grow anything in the sandy soil of West Texas and she never had the time to tackle the job. Admiring Zebulon Cooper's yard, she wondered how *he* had time to do all of this.

From a distance the dogs didn't look too big, but now that they were closer she saw the broad expanse of their chests. Had those fluffy tails not been wagging so hard or had they seemed aggressive at all, she'd be tempted to get back into her car.

"Howdy!"

She turned at the sound of the man's voice. Bending to pet the yellow dog that came directly to her, she watched Brittany greet the guy with a smile.

"Hi, Isom, how's it going? "Brittany hugged him.

"Pretty good, Brittany. You?"

"Great. I want you to meet someone."

Oddly, Emily didn't feel the need to retreat when the older man approached in his worn out cowboy hat, tattered jeans and denim shirt. His eyes were faded blue, happy and very kind. It looked as if he'd led a hard life and she liked him already. His wide smile made her feel at ease.

Isom offered Emily a handshake. "You must be Miss Emily. Blue Boy told me all about you."

"Blue Boy?"

Taking off his hat, Isom replied, "Sorry, Miss Emily, Blue is what I call Zebulon. Have since he was a little tike."

Zeb's blue eyes entered her memory. The name fit him perfectly. "Oh, I see. I like it."

"Need me to help you get somethin' out of the car?"

She only brought a few things, hoping this ordeal would end soon and she could return to her apartment. "If you'd like, you can get the big suitcase. Brittany and I can get the rest."

When the yellow dog kept biding for her attention, she reached down and petted its head again then put the key in the lock on the trunk of her red Chevrolet Cobalt. It opened with a click when she turned the key.

She felt something wet on her leg. Looking down, she saw the yellow lab licking her, so she gently pushed the dog away but her touch seemed to make it want more. "Which one is this?" she asked, patting the friendly pooch.

"That's Earl. She likes you, I can tell."

Isom grabbed the largest of the three bags, she handed one of the remaining ones to Brittany then she took the last one and closed the trunk lid. Brittany seemed almost giddy as they entered the medium-sized house. Earl forced her way in, tail wagging full speed.

The living room was decorated in western fashion. To her surprise it was warm, maybe even... inviting. Southwestern art hung on the walls and had been tastefully placed. An array of cowboy boot knickknacks sat atop the roughhewn mantle. Some looked ceramic, others wood and metal. Did he collect them?

Straight in front of them was a large archway which led into the kitchen. It was bright and clean from where she stood. She glanced to her left and through an open door. Zebulon's bedroom. A pair of jeans lay over the back of a comfortable looking chair that sat in a corner. Two pair of boots sat on the floor beside a funny wooden boot jack.

Her breath came faster. She hadn't seen one of them since her uncle threw one through the wall, barely missing her Aunt Ruby's head. She shook the thought. It was stupid to let those memories invade her mind. It had been years ago and that time in her life was over. However, seeing these things that had been familiar to her in 'not so wonderful times' lit embers of fear she'd tried to extinguish. She only hoped being here didn't kindle the fire and make it rage even worse.

CHAPTER TEN

Emily fought the need to run away. She had to remember Zebulon wasn't like that man. She glanced forward. The stairs leading to the second floor lay just beyond the door. Isom had already reached the top, turned to the right and was out of sight. Brittany was halfway up when she glanced back at her just as she forced herself to take the first step.

"I'm really excited to show you your room. It's so cool!"

"I can't wait." She watched the dog bound up the stairs.

"Well, don't sound so enthused."

Her nerves were on end with a mixture of trepidation and exhilaration. Being under the roof with Zeb was bittersweet. Knowing he would be sleeping at the bottom of the stairway should comfort her, but she was anything but calm.

She stopped at the top of the stairs. There was a quaint, average sized sitting area with a slanted ceiling, just in front of the stairs. One large window at the end of the room and one small one in the wall on one side cast light throughout the space.

Turning to the right, directly across from the waist-high railing of the stairs, was a huge wardrobe built into the wall with drawers beneath and storage cabinets on one end. Isom standing in the doorway of a room in front of her drew her attention.

"Miss Emily, if you need anything I'll be a shout away." He put his hat on his head. "Right now, I'd better get back to feedin' the horses." He turned toward the dog who had taken a place on the floor. "Come on, Earl."

She had to smile when the dog laid her head down on her paws. That K-9 wasn't going anywhere. Isom apparently knew that and didn't try to coax her.

"Guess she wants to stay."

He nodded when he passed Emily in the hall, his boot heels clicked against the wooden stairs as he descended.

"Come on, Emily. Look at your room."

"I'm coming. Hold your pants on." As soon as she went through the doorway, the room felt like home. The look on her face must have told Brittany how she felt.

"See, I told you."

She loved antiques and this room was filled with them. A cherry-wood four-poster bed sat in the middle of the far wall, a window on each side. The chest of drawers, dressing table and a small desk that sat in the corner, all matched the bed. A love seat rested at the foot of the bed and the comfortable chair in the corner with a matching foot rest complimented everything perfectly.

Antique wooden picture frames protected old photos that were hung on the seafoam green walls of the room. The beautiful hardwood floor held an area rug beneath the bed, while cheerful, white eyelet lace curtains, that matched the white eyelet quilt on the bed, covered the windows. "It's beautiful." Admiration beamed from her new, young friend's eyes.

"Isn't it, though? This was my grandmother's room." She touched the cover on top of the bed. "She made this quilt and those window hangings."

Now Emily was totally confused. How come Brittany's grandmother's room was in Zebulon's house? She put down her bag, sat on the loveseat and studied her surroundings. "I don't understand."

Brittany giggled. "Oh, sorry. I forgot you've only known us for a short while." She sat beside Emily. "My dad's grandparents built this place about seventy-five years ago. It was always a farm until Zeb got it. He's the one who made it into this sweet little ranch. Anyway, after they passed, my grandparents moved into it. Then Granddad died and Granny stayed here until she got a stomach ache one day. The ambulance rushed her to the hospital but it was too late. She had a massive heart attack. None of us got to say goodbye."

"Oh, that's so sad."

"Losing her was very heartbreaking, but she

knew we loved her. And I know she loved me, so that made it somewhat easier. Granny was a wonderful lady. I treasured coming here to spend weekends with her. Sometimes Zeb would come out to help in the fields and tend the livestock with Isom."

"Really?"

"Sure. Ole Isom's been around a long time. After Granddad was gone, Granny hired him to help around here." She smiled. "Funny, Mom and Dad always thought there was something between them."

Emily got up and began to look at the old photos on the walls. The aged wedding picture of a couple from the early nineteen-hundreds caught her eye. The groom was handsome, but the bride was absolutely stunning. "Why did they think that?"

"It's gross to imagine my granny..." She formed her fingers into quotation marks and said, "'doing it'."

"Brittanyyy." She drew her name out to make a point. "You shouldn't talk like that. She was a woman and he is a man. It's natural."

"But old people? Yuck!"

She chuckled. This girl was something else. "So, you didn't tell me why your folks thought your granny and Isom were..." She mocked Brittany. "*Doing* it."

Brittany joined Emily at the wall of photos. "Because sometimes we'd get here *early* in the morning and his truck would be parked in the same spot as the day before."

"So?"

"And he'd be at the kitchen table having coffee with Granny."

"So?"

"Uhhh, she'd be in her robe?"

Emily couldn't stifle the laugh that escaped her and heard her friend join in. As soon as she caught her breath she said, "Because she was sitting at the kitchen table in her robe, with a man, having coffee, it meant they were having an affair?"

"Eewwwwww, don't say that word."

Giving her a hard time was fun for a change. "What? Affair?"

Brittany made a gagging sound. "I think I'm going to be sick. Let's change the subject."

She focused on the pictures once again. How she'd dreamed of having a wall like this. "I wish I knew who my family was, or if I still have someone... somewhere." Brittany had a sympathetic look on her face and she was embarrassed she said anything. Why had she let that slip out? She didn't want anyone to feel sorry for her.

"Your aunt is family."

"Yes, and she's wonderful."

"What happened to your mother, and your father leaving isn't your fault."

"Well, my dad–?"

"What a bastard." Brittany met her gaze. "Who cares if you ever hear from him again?"

She shook her head. "I guess nobody but me. I've kind of accepted he didn't want me."

"Man, that sucks."

"Tell me about it. Just think how you'd feel if

you knew your father didn't love you and figured it would be easier to run away." Enough reminiscing about her family for one evening. "Okay, now I want to talk about something else."

There was one thing she'd been wondering since Brittany said this was her grandmother's room. "Tell me, if this home was in your family so long, why is Zeb living here?"

"My dad and his dad have been lifelong friends. They went through school together, graduated together and everything. Daddy decided to take a break before going to law school, so he joined the army for a few years. David, well, Mr. Cooper, went to college right out of high school. Once he got into law school he met Liz, they married, had Zebulon then Jennifer—"

"Hey, anyone up there?"

Emily's spine stiffened at the deep sound of Zeb's voice coming from the lower level. Her heart raced when she heard him climbing the stairs. Closer, closer. Her hands became clammy and she turned toward the doorway. Was she really going to stay in the house alone with this man? Had she really agreed to such a plan?

"Brittany? Em?"

Brittany walked toward the door. "We're in Granny's room."

The nearer his footsteps got, the harder she found it to breathe, then he stepped into the room. Her breath was taken away at the sight of him. What had happened to the cowboy attire he'd had on at the office that morning? It was as if a totally different person stood in front of her.

"Well," Brittany said. "You're all dressed up."

"Yeah, I had to go to court today to testify for one of my clients. He got his divorce, the kids and the kicker is his ex has to pay child support."

"Serves her right."

Emily couldn't take her eyes off the man. He wore a dark blue suit that brought out the color of his eyes. Highly polished black shoes and a hounds tooth multi-colored tie. His hair, combed back on top away from his face showing his full features, curled against his collar. She longed to run her fingers through the sleek and shininess of it. Sexy from head to toe. At that moment, no one would have guessed he was a cowboy. In reality, he was just a man, so why couldn't she get past the other part?

The moment he walked through the door of the upstairs bedroom, Zeb noticed Emily looked like she belonged. Hell, she looked like she belonged anywhere, especially with him. He'd never seen her with her hair pulled back. Her neck was long, inviting and he'd love to put his lips on it and kiss all the way down to her toes.

Brittany greeted Zebulon with a hug. "I was just telling Emily the story behind why you own Granny's house now."

"Oh, I see. Well, don't let me stop you. Go on." He took a seat on the overstuffed chair in the corner, loosened his tie, stretched his legs out in front of him then propped his feet on the hassock. This room was one of his favorites. Sometimes he'd come up here just to relax. It was the freshest space in the house and it reminded him of old Granny Mills.

He glanced over at Emily. Why was she staring at him? "See something you like?" He could kick himself in the ass for saying out loud what he'd been thinking, but it was too late now. He watched her brow furrow. She was even beautiful when she frowned.

"Pardon me? I didn't hear you. What did you say?"

The look on her face said she was telling the truth and he was glad for it. Maybe he could get out of sticking his foot in his mouth. "I said it's something I like."

"What?" She glanced around the room.

"Um, this house. I like it. No, actually, I love it." He could tell by the way Brittany was glaring at him that she *had* heard what he'd said. "Right, Brittany?" For a moment he wondered if she was going to keep his secret.

"I have to admit, you do love this house as much as my family does. Anyway, let me finish telling you about it, Emily."

"Okay, I'm anxious to hear the rest of the story."

"Let's see, where did I leave off?"

"The Cooper's got married and had their kids."

"Oh, yeah. So, anyway…" Brittany glanced at her watch. "Is it already six o'clock? I have to go. I have a date coming to pick me up at seven." She looked at Zeb. "You can finish telling her why you live here."

The two women hugged and he wondered what would happen if he pulled Emily in his arms and hugged her like that. She'd probably slap the hell out of him. He smiled at the thought.

Brittany straightened and started toward the doorway. "Okay, I'll see you when all this stuff's straightened out. Bye bye."

He pulled his feet from the stool, stood and watched her walk out the door. "Bye. Be careful driving. Don't be in too big of a hurry. That date's not as important as your life." He saw the young woman roll her eyes. It was typical for Brittany.

"Oh, please, Zebulon, stop. You worry about taking care of Emily and I'll worry about taking care of me." She turned toward Emily. "Sometimes he acts like the big brother I never had."

He lunged at Brittany like he was going to chase her and spoke in a low menacing voice, "You'd better get outta here. Ruuun!"

"Ahhhhh," she screamed and ran.

He heard Brittany's footsteps descending the stairs and enjoyable laughter coming from behind him. Turning, he saw total amusement on Emily's pretty face. He'd never seen her laugh before and it became her. "I like tormenting that girl."

"I can see that." She stopped laughing and met his gaze. "She thinks a lot of you."

"I feel the same way about her."

"Would you finish telling me about the house?"

"Simple truth is, after Granny Mills died, Bob and Liz didn't care to live here but they didn't want a stranger to have it. I'd always loved the place, and I'd been a trooper for eight years then was accepted as a ranger, so I had a good income. I met—" No, he wasn't going to tell her about finding and losing the woman he'd thought was the one of his dreams. Now, as he looked at Emily, he realized he might have been wrong. Curiosity flashed in her eyes and he knew the question was coming.

"You're a Texas Ranger?"

It wasn't the question he expected, but this was one he could handle better than having to tell her about Jasmine. Then again, could he tell her the truth about why he left the department?

CHAPTER ELEVEN

Emily waited for Zebulon to answer, but before he did, she noted a brief sadness in his eyes. She couldn't help but wonder what caused it.

"Not anymore."

"Why not?" She shouldn't be asking this man personal questions but the way he made her heart flutter was something new and she found herself wanting to know more about him.

"It's a long story."

He was avoiding the question, so she let it drop. Maybe someday, after they knew each other better, he'd tell her. "I see. So, back to the reason you live here then?" His smile warmed her heart and she longed to touch his cheek, which now was whiskered with a five o'clock shadow.

"Yes, I think that's a good idea. I brought some

Chinese home for our supper. Let me get out of this suit then I'll meet you in the kitchen in ten minutes and tell you all about it."

If the butterflies in her stomach flapped their wings any faster, she'd start floating on air. The thought of having an intimate meal with him, one on one, gave her nerves a twist but what could she say? No? That wasn't going to happen. "Okay, I think I'll change from my work clothes, too."

"Sounds good." He turned and walked toward the door. "See you in a few."

She closed the door and opened her suitcase. What would she wear? Jeans? Shorts? Tank top? T-shirt? What was wrong with her? Unbuttoning her blouse, she realized she wanted to dress in something she thought Zeb would like, but she didn't have a western shirt and cowboy boots, nor did she intend to ever own any. Shorts and a t-shirt would have to do.

Before she went down, she studied the living area at the top of the stairs more closely. There was a flat screen T.V., a matching couch and chair, a computer desk with papers spread out across the top in front of the screen, a filing cabinet and printer. She totally missed these things before. Was this his office? She was hoping this area would be hers and would keep them separated most of the time, but if he was up here working then—"

"Hey, you comin'?"

Damn, she almost jumped out of her skin. "On my way." Before she reached the bottom of the stairs, she smelled the enticing aroma of the food and her stomach growled. She hadn't realized how hungry she was. Upon entering the kitchen she saw Zeb was once again in his jeans and cowboy boots, but this time, it didn't bother her. She actually kind of liked it. Now, that was really amazing.

She glanced around the spacious area. The cabinets had glass fronts and everything was neatly organized behind them. The room was separated by an island with a breakfast bar. The natural wood table and four chairs, which sat in a nook of a large bay window, looked handmade. It was rustic, yet inviting. Three stools that matched the dining set were at the bar where Zebulon already had their places set and the food, enough for an army, ready to dish out.

"Smells yummy."

"Good. Hope you like chicken chow mien."

"Love it." He couldn't have known it was her favorite, but it was.

"How about egg drop soup, fried rice, egg rolls and crab Rangoon's?"

She took her seat. "Did you buy out the restaurant?"

"No, but I'm so hungry, everything looked good."

"I'm starving, too."

"Then dig in. It's gettin' cold."

She spooned helpings onto her plate and wondered why she was so at ease at the moment. It felt right being here, which surprised her. She'd gotten a lot of surprises that day. Finding out Zebulon was Mr. Cooper's son, who lived in the Mills' house, who liked chicken chow mien, who used to be a Texas Ranger, who looked like a million bucks in a dark blue suit, who was sitting so close to her she felt his body heat and it was doing things to her she'd never experienced. What a day.

"I wanted to buy it." Zebulon took a drink of tea.

"Buy what, the Chinese food?"

"No, goofy, this house."

"Oh, duh!" She should have known what he was talking about. That's what they'd been discussing earlier. He laughed, she supposed at herself-chiding. Whatever it was, she liked the sound of his laughter. It made her smile. "And don't call me goofy, he's a dog." She met his gaze and she could swear she saw passion simmering in the depths of his azure eyes.

"You're no dog. You're a beautiful woman, Emily." He glanced down at his plate then back at Emily. "I'm sorry, that was inappropriate."

His words were apologetic, but his eyes told a different story. Her heart beat wildly in her chest and she wondered if he could hear its cadence. This was crazy. How could he affect her like this? The look on his face told her he was having the same feelings. The moment was awkward, but at the same time exhilarating. "No, really, I appreciate the compliment."

Turning her attention back to her food, she asked, "So did you?"

"Did I what?"

"Buy the house?"

"Oh, duh!"

His belly laugh was contagious and she joined in. It lightened the desire that had just passed between them and she became at ease again. "Now who's goofy?"

"Touché. Yes, I bought it. I've been coming here since I was a boy. Mr. and Mrs. Mills were like my own grandparents and I loved them very much. Granddad M would let me come out and ride his horses all the time. He also made me help with the farming, though. I had to do some work around here. That's part of the reason I have always felt at home."

She watched him look lovingly around the room. "So that's why you made it your home?"

He swallowed the bite of food he'd taken. "Pretty much. Plus I thought it would be perfect for me and—"

Why did he always stop in mid-sentence? There was something he was holding back and whatever it was is what brought the sadness to his eyes. "And?"

This woman made him want to talk about Jasmine and what happened. But why? He knew the answer. He was comfortable with her and compelled to share his problems, his life. Yet he barely knew her.

"And..." He pointed to her plate. "Are you done?"

"You're changing the subject again. And who, what?"

He'd gone too far to turn back now. Maybe he should tell her and get it over with. "You're right, I am." He peered into her emerald eyes. She was a beauty. "Are you sure you want to know?"

"I'm sure."

"Then let's get this cleaned up and go in the living room. I'll tell you all—" He turned at the sound of the dogs barking. "What the hell's wrong with them?" He hadn't heard them bark that frantically in a long time. Was someone out there?

He ran to his room, grabbed his Khar CW-40 semi-automatic pistol, and headed for the back door where the commotion was coming from. He glanced back at Emily, her expression more curiosity than concern. "Go upstairs and wait for me. Do *not* come outside. Hear me?" Her affirmative nod was his answer. He only hoped he could trust her to do what she said she would.

Opening the door, he glanced around the property. No strange vehicles were in sight. Dusk was a hard time of day to see, but he could make out that the dogs had something, or someone cornered around the side of the barn.

Gun in hand and ready to shoot, he zigzagged his way across the yard and flattened himself against the barn wall. He inched his way toward the barking dogs then heard yelp… yelp… yelp. Had someone kicked one of them? Another yelp and he started to rush the scene, but Buck came running around the corner of the barn in his direction before he could do it. In the last light of day, he saw what had happened. Quills stuck this way and that out of the dog's muzzle. "A porcupine."

Oh, no. Not again. He dropped his hands to his side and went to the other side of the barn. Earlene continued to bark. "Earl, get over here before you get too close. Didn't you see what happened to Buck?" The dog quieted but continued to sniff at the rodent. "Earl! Get! I'm going to try to get this thing out of here." As slow as the blasted things moved, he might be there all night.

A snigger from behind him gave him a start. He whirled and brought his gun up ready to defend himself.

"It's me. Don't shoot."

There stood Emily with a cast iron skillet in her hand. "What the hell do you think you're doing?"

"I couldn't just stay in there while you put your life on the line. What if you'd needed help?"

"Do you know how stupid it was of you to come out here?"

"Stupid? I was just trying to help." She put her hands on her hips. "I'd appreciate it if you don't call me stupid."

He closed his eyes and silently counted to ten. Soon he'd have to get it through to her that she may really be in danger and when he told her to do something, she needed to do it. It could mean the difference in life or death. For both of them, but now wasn't the time. "I'm sorry. You startled me, that's all."

Standing there with her hands on her shapely hips, holding the frying pan, she looked gorgeous. The full moon made her hair glow golden brown in its light and her eyes flashed with yellow sparks of anger. He couldn't conceal the smile that lifted the corners of his mouth. Placing his gun beneath his belt, in the small of his back, he watched her glare at him. "What?" He held his hands out in a questioning gesture. "I said I'm sorry." Unable to stifle the laugh any longer, he let it all out then saw the twinkle in her eye. She raised the frying pan in the air as if she intended to hit him with it.

Emily began to giggle. She must look a sight standing there holding a cast iron skillet in the air. How could this man make her laugh so spontaneously? "You are incorrigible." She saw something move at Zebulon's feet. Her eyes widened at the sight of the thing. "Look out."

As fast as her feet would carry her, she ran to where he was standing and put the pan between Zebulon's leg and the porcupine's quills just before they came in contact. Zeb quickly moved out of the way and the hilarity of the moment hit them again. She couldn't remember laughing that hard in a long time.

"May I borrow that?" He nodded toward the pan.

"Sure." Trying to catch her breath was impossible. Not from laughing, but from the heat the brush of his fingers on hers left behind. For a brief moment their gazes met and he was so close she thought he was going to kiss her. He cleared his throat and backed away. She should have known he didn't want to kiss her. Why did she torture herself like that? He was a cowboy so why should she care?

"We'd better get this thing away from the house before someone else gets stuck." He bent and placed the pan behind the porcupine. "Come on, dude, let's go."

She turned to go back into the house. If nothing else, she could hide in her room until he left in the morning. The sound of his voice calling her stopped her in her tracks.

"Hey! Will you help me in a few minutes?"

Twisting her neck to the side, without looking

back she said, "Help with what?"

"I have to get those quills out of Buck's snout. I'll need some help. Meet me in the barn. Please?"

The *please* was a question. Just then Buck trotted up in front of her, whining as if he knew what his master had asked. How could she turn him down, but the barn? The horses were in there. The porch light illuminated the poor dog's condition. Another whimper came from the pitiful creature and her heart melted. "Okay, I'll help."

"Thanks."

Earlene scampered up beside her and the other dog and began to lick at Buck's ears. Did she feel sorry for her friend? "I know, Earl. He looks like hell, doesn't he?" She hoped her stomach would take pulling the spines out of Buck's nose. She'd never done anything like that before, but it looked as if she was about to.

Facing her fear of horses was another thing she was about to do. She glanced down at the injured pup. "Dang it, Buck. Why'd you have to do this my first night here?"

CHAPTER TWELVE

The barn lights were bright and the smell of leather, horses and hay played with Emily's senses. She stuck her head inside the door to see if Zeb was already there. She didn't hear anything. She wasn't going inside until he got there.

"Boo!"

She jumped and whirled around, her fisted hand flew through the air, but just before the blow landed, Zeb grabbed her wrist. Her heart pounded and the lump that had formed in her throat wasn't going away. "Damn, you scared me half to death." Her arm tingled where his fingers wrapped around her skin and he made her feel very much alive.

"Has anyone ever told you how great you look in cutoffs and a t-shirt?"

The pan clanked on the ground and his fingers grasp her other wrist. "Not lately." His voice was husky and he stepped closer. He pulled her arms up and placed them around his neck, then dropped his behind her back and pulled her even nearer. The spicy smell that was uniquely Zebulon toyed with her emotions.

The immediacy of his body pressed against hers made her feel as if she'd swoon. Or was it his eyes, intense with want? He wanted her? How could that be when only minutes ago he'd... no, she didn't want to think about that now. She wanted to savor the moment.

"Well, you do."

"I-I guess I should say thank—" His mouth met hers and she leaned into him. First the kiss was gentle, then he lined her mouth with his tongue and she opened for him. The caress deepened until she thought she would melt into one with him, then he pulled back. She wanted this to last longer, but it was over. He continued to hold her and she couldn't open her eyes. If she did, she'd be back in reality.

"Damn, girl. What you do to me."

If Emily only knew how many sensations she brought out in him. It was going to be hard to stay away from this enticing woman. He didn't want to, but it was something he had to do. If he let his feelings get in the way of protecting her, he might make a mistake, but for some reason, she was fragile. Either she'd been hurt in the past, or she'd never known the love of a man. Either way, he was going to try to protect her heart and her life.

"What, tell me?"

Her voice was barely above a whisper. There

was something he read behind her eyes. Naivety? Could that be it?

No matter how hard he tried, he couldn't stop himself from telling her the truth. "You make me want you." Her actions were pure and her body trembled against him.

"Really?"

"Yes." All he wanted to do was take her to his bed and make love to her all night, and something about her actions told him *she* wanted it. However, he had to put a stop to this before it went any further. For her sake, and his. Thankfully, Buck and Earl came up behind him. The dogs' panting and Buck's whine reminded him of why they were there.

The last thing he wanted to do was let her go, but it was the first thing he *had* to do. He took his arms from around her waist and reached to pull hers from around his neck. Damn he missed her warmth when they stepped apart. "I think Buck needs our attention." This was going to be a hard few days. He needed to solve the mystery of who was stalking this beautiful woman fast. He had to keep his hands off her at all costs or her life wouldn't be the only thing in danger.

Emily's hormones raged with primal instinct. Why had he stopped so abruptly? She didn't want the kiss to end and was shocked at the emotions that flitted through her when it did. Then a horse whinnied in the background and the passion that possessed her only seconds ago fled, and she stiffened. "C-can that horse get out?" She saw a questioning frown mark Zeb's brow.

"No, why?"

He walked deeper into the barn but she stayed where she was by the door. If she had to run, this would be the safest place. "Are you sure?" She watched him walk back toward her. Her heart pounded in her chest, but this time it was from fear. The fear of having to go inside.

"Are you afraid of horses?"

She swallowed hard and drew a calming breath. "Y-yes. I have been since I was a little girl."

"Is that why you're hesitating to come inside?"

Unable to speak she nodded. He approached and took her hand. His touch reassured her and she appreciated it, but she also knew she had to go into the barn.

"I promise, none of the horses can get out of their stalls. They won't hurt you." He smiled. "Matter of fact. Where we're going to go to take the quills out of Buck's face isn't even near the stalls. Come on."

The tug on her hand helped to propel her forward. She didn't want to look around the barn, but couldn't help herself. It was big and bright and not at all like the dark and dirty one her uncle Able kept his horses in. One of the equines snorted and she jumped then felt Zebulon squeeze her hand.

"It's okay. We're going right in here."

She followed him into a room where a waist-high wooden table sat in the middle. Bridles, spurs, horseshoes, ropes and other tack hung on the walls. It smelled of leather. It smelled, well, good and she couldn't believe it.

"Are you going to be all right?"

The rhythm of her heart started to slow. This wasn't so bad after all, but she wasn't near the horses either. "I think so. Yes." He released her hand but the warmth of his touch lingered, just as his taste remained on her lips. She'd never been kissed like that and longed to experience it again.

"Buck! Come 'ere, boy."

Both dogs came in the tack room and Zebulon closed the door. She dreaded the pain they were about to inflict on the dog, but it had to be done. "At least he didn't get too many quills in him."

"Yes, but taking them out isn't going to be pleasant no matter how few there are. Come on, buddy, let's get this over with."

From Buck's size, she'd say he probably weighed over a hundred pounds and Zebulon lifted him onto the table with little effort. He was strong, handsome and all man. "Poor guy."

"Yep, that's for sure. We'll take these out tonight then I'll take him to the vet in the morning to make sure we got everything. Quills are strange things. They have little barbs on them that go one way. If you don't get them all out, they'll work their way in deeper." He reached for some pliers. "If they get inside the body, they can puncture an organ."

"But they're only in his face."

"He was lucky, looks like there are only seven of them and they're not too deep. We're going to need to protect our hands. We don't want to get stuck with these things."

She met his gaze and he handed her some gloves. She put them on then noticed he held a pair of needle nose pliers out for her to take. Did he expect her to do this? "I can't pull those out." His smile was mischievous and she was tempted to slap it off his handsome face.

"You think you can hold him down and comfort him while *I* pull them out?"

There was no way she could manhandle that hulk of a dog. "Well, I—" The metal tool felt awkward through the thick leather of the gloves. This was crazy. She had never experienced anything like this in her life. But then, she wouldn't have thought she'd be in a barn with a cowboy ever again either.

"That's what I thought. Now you have to be careful because those things can break off, so when you get ready to pull one out, put the plier as close to his fur as possible, then pull with slow, steady pressure."

"What if I hurt him?"

"Oh, it's going to hurt alright, but he's a tough guy. He'll holler and wail, but he'll be okay."

The knot in her stomach tightened, but she had to help Buck. "Okay, I'm ready." When she knew Zebulon had a firm grip on the K-9 she grasped the first quill with the plier and pulled. It was harder than she thought it would be but she continued to apply steady pressure even when Buck yelped as the spike came out.

"Hey, you're a natural at this."

She felt anything but comfortable. "Yeah, right. I just know it has to be done, so I'm going to do my best."

The second quill came out a little easier and by the time she got to the last one, she had the procedure down pretty well. Zebulon let the dog go, picked up the quills and threw them in a large trash barrel. The lap of a warm tongue wet her cheek and made her smile.

"Would you look at that. He's saying thanks."

The dog continued to lick her face and she batted at him with her gloved hands. "You're welcome already. Stop." Even though their first encounter was painful, it was nice to know she was appreciated by her new found friend.

"Okay, bud, that's enough. She loves you, too." Zeb lifted the dog off the table and opened the door. "Thanks for the help. You were a trooper."

"Thanks." She pulled off the gloves and handed them to him. The word trooper reminded her of their earlier conversation about law enforcement and buying the house. "You want to finish telling me who or what... *and* is?" His words chilled her to the bone and bile rose in her throat as she watched him walk out of the room.

"Jasmine, my fiancée."

CHAPTER THIRTEEN

Emily's heart dropped to the pit of her stomach. How could he have kissed her like that knowing he belonged to another woman? She hurried out of the barn behind him. "That's it? That's all, just my fiancée? You're engaged?" His tall frame silhouetted in the light glowing from the back porch. His shoulders weren't as squared as usual. Then, to her surprise, he stopped but didn't turn around.

"Not anymore."

She almost breathed a sigh of relief, but the hurt in his voice said he wasn't over the woman he called Jasmine and her heart went out to him. She knew what it was like to be hurt. Not by someone she'd been in love with, but someone she loved nonetheless. He started toward the house again and she ran to catch up. Putting her hand on his shoulder, she gently pulled back and he stopped at her touch. "Talk to me, cowboy." Had those words just come out of her mouth?

Zebulon turned to face Emily. "Let's sit down."

She heard the pain that riddled his voice then watched when he pointed to a table and chairs that decorated the deck on the side of the house. It sat in the shadows and she wondered if it was going to be easier for him to talk to her in the dark. She followed him and took the chair opposite from where he sat.

The full moon was rising higher in the sky and she saw the hurt look on his face. "What happened?" She asked the question, though she wasn't sure she wanted to hear about his love for another woman. What difference did it make? She didn't have a claim on the man. However, her feelings for him were growing and she didn't know how bad it would hurt to hear what he had to say.

"This is hard for me to talk about." He met her gaze.

His eyes glowed like a sapphire in the light of the moon. His discomfort evident, she longed to go to him and soothe him. "Yes, I can tell. If you don't want to, I understand."

"No, I said I'd tell you." He took a breath and let it out. "To become a Texas Ranger in the Division, it's required you have an outstanding record with a bonified law enforcement agency for at least eight years. Right out of high school I got a job with the Texas Department of Public Safety. I worked hard and became a commissioned officer ranked a trooper II. You have to be an officer to become a ranger. Anyway, like I told you, I was a trooper for eight years then was accepted into the division. That's what I wanted to do all my life. Being a Texas Ranger, well, law enforcement, meant everything to me."

"How long were you a ranger?"

"Not long."

The sadness in his eyes broke her heart. What was behind the sorrow? His smile didn't hide his hurt.

"One of my days as a trooper, I stopped a young lady for speeding down a county road. Her name was Jasmine Dade. Her smile brightened my day. I noticed she wasn't wearing a wedding ring and I wanted to ask her for her number, but that was against the rules so I gave her a warning and let her go.

"Next day at the office, my friend Andy yelled to me that I had a phone call. It was her. She'd gotten my name off the warning ticket and wanted to meet me for lunch or a drink."

Never in her entire life had Emily even contemplated calling a man and asking him out. However, if she'd been the woman in that car, she may have done the same thing.

Zeb couldn't believe he was telling Emily about Jasmine. He hadn't talked about it before, and now he was spilling everything. In the past, when he'd thought of Jasmine, he believed he'd never love again, but the woman sitting in front of him had him all torn up inside. He wondered if he was falling in love with her. If he loved her, it would be a deeper love than he'd ever had.

"So, we met. I'll spare you the details of our relationship, but I decided I was in love and asked her to marry me." He met Emily's gaze. Jasmine had been pretty, but this woman was beautiful. He wished he knew what she was thinking, how she felt about him. Hopefully, the things he was telling her wouldn't hurt her. That was the last thing he wanted to do.

"And she said yes, didn't she."

He nodded and tried to read her expression, but he couldn't. "I bought this place before I met her, but thought it would be a great place to live after we married. She, however, had other ideas. She wanted to live in town and I just couldn't bring myself to give the place up. Finally she agreed to live out here for a while so we began planning the wedding.

His heart leaped into his throat when he thought about how it all ended. He couldn't tell Emily that he'd made love to Jasmine the night before he'd lost her and that he'd left only an hour before he got the call. No, he'd spare Emily those details.

"It was a rainy Monday morning. I had just started my shift and a call came in that there'd been an accident. I was already in my patrol car and started for the site."

"Oh, my God. It was her, wasn't it?"

"Yes, it was. She never had a chance. A drunk driver in a 4x4 truck broadsided her. She never knew what hit her."

"I'm so sorry." She got up and started around the table.

He held up his hand to stop her. "No, please,

sympathy only makes it worse, but thank you." After she sat back down he realized what he really wanted was for her to come to him, sit in his lap, put her arms around him and hold him. But that wouldn't be fair to her. Not while he was talking about another woman. Would it?

Images of Jasmine's blood flowing with the rain into the gutter seemed to flash before his eyes. That gray day tainted with red was imprinted on his mind but he wanted nothing more than to move past the memory. Live again. Love again. He studied Emily, could this woman be the answer?

"Is that why you quit the department?"

"Yeah, that day I decided I never wanted to come up on a scene like that again. It hurt too bad."

"Yes, but it was someone you loved. If that had been a stranger, it would have been hard, but you would have just done your job."

"I've thought of that a million times, but it doesn't change the fact that I quit." He wasn't a quitter, never had been, but that day he walked off from a job he valued and never returned.

"It's never too late to go back."

"It's too late for me."

"So you'd rather be a private investigator than a ranger?"

"Never in a million years. But... it's what I chose and I'll stick with it." He stood and started inside. "Speaking of investigating, I have some of that to do tomorrow on a new case I started today." He walked over to Emily and pulled her to her feet. "A friend of mine is being stalked."

The scent of cherry blossoms wafted from her

hair. She smelled so good and she was so soft. "Can I have that hug now?"

~ ~ ~

Emily lay awake and watched the moonlight dance through the open window of her temporary room. She couldn't get Zebulon off her mind. The feel of his arms around her on the deck, the kiss in the barn lingered on her lips, his unique spicy scent invaded her memory. It all felt right and wrong at the same time.

Her emotion climbed, curved and spiraled down. Her heart and mind were on a roller coaster. One thing she knew, she liked Zeb Cooper too much for her own good. If a woman could fall in love after just meeting someone, she feared it was happening to her.

He needed to solve this case fast. She glanced out the window. Out there, her life was in danger. In here, she peered around the room, it was her heart. She turned to Earlene who lay on the bed beside her. The dog refused to leave her and it was nice to have the company. "Earl, what am I going to do? I can't fall for your master. He's been in love and I think he was hurt enough that he won't do it again."

She thought she'd never go to sleep, but as it always did, slumber prevailed in the early hours of morning. When she awoke, bright sunlight streamed through the window, Earlene was gone and her bedroom door was wide open. She knew she'd closed it the night before.

Glancing at the bedside clock, she was

astonished. "Eleven o'clock?" She pulled back the covers and left the coziness of the bed. She hadn't slept this late since she was a teenager. The rest must have been well needed.

A private bathroom adjoined her room and a shower sounded fabulous. She realized now that she had to relieve herself. That must have been why her door was open. Zeb had let Earlene out to use the bathroom. The thought that he might have been watching her while she slept excited her. She only hoped she didn't have her mouth open.

The bathroom was small, bright and clean, like the other rooms in the house. Either Zeb was a heck of a housekeeper or someone came and cleaned for him periodically.

She showered and dressed then started downstairs. Zeb had probably gone to town to his office to work. At least she assumed he had an office. That meant she was alone in the house. Until she heard the steady rhythm of a squeaking noise and just as fast as it had started, it subsided. She was surprised to see Earl meet her at the bottom of the stairs.

"Well, where'd you come from, ladybug?" The dog's wagging tail made her smile. "Let's see if we can find me something to eat." As soon as she got into the kitchen, she noticed the large dog door. That must have been the source of the squeaking. Why hadn't she seen that the night before?

The coffee pot was still on and she longed for a nice hot cup of it. Once it was poured she took a sip. "Mmmm. Now I think a bowl of cereal sounds really good." She opened one cabinet door after the other until she found three boxes of different kinds of breakfast cereal. It was almost noon, but she still wanted breakfast. "I've never told anyone this before, Earl, but sometimes I have breakfast at supper time."

"So do I."

She twirled to meet the blue-eyed man's gaze. Buck stood by his side. "Oh, hi, I didn't know you were home."

"I just got back from taking my buddy here to the vet. The man said you did a good job de-quilling him."

She turned back to making her breakfast. "Thanks, maybe I should change my profession."

"So, did you get all the beauty rest you needed?"

"Don't be a smart ass." Truth was, she thought the reason she slept so long, once she went to sleep, was because she felt comfortable and safe under the same roof as him.

"And I see you took your feisty pill, too."

Taking the strawberries out of the fridge, she shot him a look she hoped told him she didn't think he was very funny. "I'm making myself at home, I hope that's okay."

He popped a berry in his mouth. "I wouldn't have it any other way."

"Didn't your mother ever tell you not to talk with your mouth full?"

"Sure she did but I didn't listen."

"No doubt." She sat at the breakfast bar and began to eat. "Have you had time to look into my case?"

Pulling the other stool from beneath the bar, he

took a seat beside Emily. "I went by the loft building and talked a little bit to Mr. Meyer. His wife didn't say much, but was pleasant and seemed very concerned."

"She's a sweetheart and so is he. Did they give you any clues?"

"He gave me some information on the maintenance man. His name's Dewey Barton. He's only been working for them about six months."

"Hmmm, that's only a few months before I moved in." She took the last bite of cereal.

"Yes, I know. I called my friend Andy and he's running a check on him to see if he has a record." He met her gaze. "I know this sounds like a stupid question, but do you have any enemies?"

"Well, there was a girl I kicked in the shin in the seventh grade. She stole a poster of my favorite country music star out of my locker."

He laughed. "That's probably not it."

"Yeah, I don't even remember her name."

"No, I mean any *real* adversaries. Someone who might think you owe them something or someone you've hurt in the past."

Her thoughts automatically went to her father and her uncle. They were the only two people in her life she knew hated her. "Yes, I do, but it's been so long since I've heard from either of them I wouldn't think—"

"No matter how long it's been, we can't rule them out. Who are these people?"

It was now or never. She would have to spill her life out to him, but it was nothing worse than what he told her last night, except neither of these two people loved her like he'd been loved by Jasmine.

"My father, and my aunt's ex-husband." There, she'd said it.

"We need to do some serious talking. Want to grab another cup of coffee and go out on the deck? It's a beautiful day out there."

"Deck talkers, that's what we are."

"Well," he said filling a cup with coffee. "I've been called worse."

She couldn't help but giggle while she followed him out the back door. "I suppose you have."

"Hey, what's that supposed to mean."

She shrugged. "Just saying." Rounding the corner that led to the large expanse of the wooden deck, she saw Isom in a corral with two horses and her stomach lurched. Why couldn't she get over being afraid? She wasn't even close to the mangy things.

"You look as if you've seen a ghost. What's wrong?"

Motioning toward the corral she took her seat. "Horses."

CHAPTER FOURTEEN

*Z*ebulon noted the squint of her eyes when she watched Isom walking the horses around the corral. "Tell me again why you're afraid of them."

"Inside, I said my uncle was one of the people in my life who didn't like me."

He nodded. "Yes." As close as he was sitting, the low neckline of the tank top she wore allowed him to see the slight pulse that beat in her throat. The pace quickened when she said the man's name.

"Able. Good ole Uncle Able." She shook her head and peered into her coffee cup.

The wheels were turning in her mind, he could tell. What had Able done to her? "What's his last name?" He took his pad and pen out of his shirt pocket. Making notes of everything while conversations were happening was the best way for him to keep track of names, places and dates. He relied on this little jewel for more than he should.

"Collins. He was a… well…"

His curiosity was piqued. "A what, an ass?"

She chuckled. "Well, that, too. But no, he was a cowboy."

"So, you don't like cowboys?"

"I didn't." She met his gaze. "Until now."

He loved the way her green eyes sparkled with flecks of yellow in the late morning sun. "Did I change your mind about the way you feel about cowboys?" *Please let her answer be yes.*

"No, Isom did."

"Oh, thanks."

She looked away and started to laugh. "No, I'm just kidding. You and Isom are both really nice guys. Able is the one who made me afraid of cowboys and horses."

"Afraid? We're just men."

"I know." She admitted. "It looks like living in Texas all my life I'd have gotten over it by now, and don't get me wrong, I'm getting better, but still…"

He reached across the table and put his hand over hers. "Look at me." Her smile faded when she gazed into his eyes. "I am one cowboy that will *never* hurt you. I can promise you the same of Isom." She nodded affirmatively. He didn't want to move his hand from hers, but touching her was a distraction. One he didn't need at the moment. Concentration is what he needed to figure out who might want to hurt this woman he was growing so fond of.

"I'm starting to figure that out, and I appreciate it. Maybe afraid isn't the right word. Dislike is probably a better term."

Her not liking cowboys definitely didn't work to his advantage. "So tell me about this ass, slash, cowboy uncle of yours." The smile that lifted the corners of her mouth said he'd lightened the mood again. The last thing he wanted was for her to be uneasy talking to him. "Was he abusive?"

"You could say that. Not so much physically to me like he was to my aunt, but he ripped me mentally. Aunt Ruby tried to protect me all she could."

Why was she around this man so much? "Did you live with these people?"

"Yes." She took a drink of coffee then set the cup back on the table. "That's kind of where my dad comes in. He caused it all. Or rather, I caused it."

What could this woman have done as a small child to think she could have prompted the behavior of adults? He couldn't imagine. "Why do you think you instigated the things that happened?" He watched her take a deep breath contemplating her answer. She let the breath out and he observed the rise and fall of her chest. Her nipples slightly showed through the thin cloth of the tank top. *Focus, dummy!* It was hard, but he forced himself to look away. Damn, she was all in his head!

Isom stood at the edge of the corral. "Hey, Blue Boy, you two want to take these horses out for a little ride? They need some exercise."

Emily's head jerked up and her eyes grew wide.

He knew the last thing this lady wanted to do was go near a horse, much less ride one, but he wanted her to answer. "Well?"

"Never. I'll never get on another horse."

That told him she'd ridden before. What had happened? He was sure he was about to learn. "Never say never, Em." It would be nice if he could take his own advice and never say never about falling in love again.

"Easy for you to say."

He waved at the older man. "Not today. Thanks, Isom." Nodding, Isom went about his business and Zeb turned his attention back to Emily. "From the beginning?"

"Well, I really don't know anything about my father except he never wanted children. Of course, I came along and my mom told me he resented the hell out of me. He stayed 'til I was three then just took off. Never to be heard from again."

"Your mom didn't talk about him or tell you about him?" The way she chuckled said it was one of hurt, not happiness.

Shaking her head, she said, "No. Matter of fact she did everything in her power *not* to tell me anything. I don't even know his name. He could be dead for all I know."

"His name's not Tipton?" He made notes as she continued to talk.

"No, that was my mother's maiden name. She changed everything. Before she died, she even went to great lengths to draw up legal papers so he couldn't contact me in any way until I was twenty-five."

Damn the tragedy this beautiful creature had endured in her lifetime. He fought the urge to pull her into his arms and hold her, ease her pain if he could. "When did your mom pass, and how?"

"When my father left, Mom turned to drugs and alcohol. I started staying more and more at Aunt Ruby's. Uncle Able was another one who didn't want me, but I had nowhere else to go. Then one Saturday morning when I was five, I got up and turned the T.V. on to watch cartoons. I waited and waited for my mother to get up. Finally, I went in her room and saw she was sleeping. Her room smelled funny. An odor I wasn't familiar with. Now, I know it was the smell of death."

"Oh, darlin', I don't know what to say."

"I've never talked about this, well about Able's abuse anyway. I told Brittany a little about my father. Other than that, none of these words have ever been spoken out loud. Not by me at least."

Things were getting too heavy. He didn't want her to get bogged down in the memories and fall into a depression. He'd seen it happen in clients before, but she was more than a client. She was becoming part of his life and he hoped it would be more than a temporary thing. "Hey, have you ever been fishin'?"

At that moment Emily was numb and hadn't realized what Zebulon said. "Huh? What?"

"Have you ever been fishin'?"

His eyes were kind and held compassion in their azure depths. "You are a master at changing the subject, aren't you?" That mischievous glint in his eye spelled trouble and she trusted whatever was behind that look would probably be fun. That was something she needed to have a little of. "No."

"Never?"

"Nope."

"Well, by golly madam I think it's about time you went."

The thought of touching a slimy fish was not one that enticed her, but being alone with Zeb was. "I'm not touching any fish."

"You will if you catch one. That's part of the deal." He stood and started toward the barn. "There's a picnic basket in the pantry. Why don't you put us something together. I'll get the four-wheeler."

"Four-wheeler?" The butterflies in her stomach were at it again. He expected her to ride behind him? His backside between her legs, her arms around his waist, her breasts against his back... the thoughts that were running through her mind were shameless, but she smiled at the prospect.

"Have you ever driven one?"

Was he crazy? She'd never even been on one. "No."

"It's easy, don't worry about it."

She opened the screen door. "Whatever you say." She wasn't afraid to try to drive one, but so much for her fantasy.

The picnic basket was packed and she heard the sound of two four-wheelers rounding the corner at the front of the house. She grabbed the basket and went outside, surprised to see one of the vehicles was gray, the other a bright pink. Isom jumped off the pink one and turned toward her.

"Have a good time, but watch Blue, he'll have you doing stunts on this thing if you're not careful." Isom headed back toward the corral. "Buck, Earl, y'all come on now, you know Blue don't like y'all traipsin' alongside when he's on that machine."

She probably already knew the answer to the question but she had to ask. "Isom?"

He stopped and the dogs stayed by his side. "Ma'am?"

"Why do you call him Blue?"

"Have you looked at his eyes, Miss Emily?"

Had she ever! She glanced at Zeb and saw a slight blush on his cheeks. Was he embarrassed? "I see your point."

She turned her attention once again to Zeb and the four-wheelers. Then she realized the pink one had probably been Jasmine's and wondered how many times the woman and Zeb had ridden them together. She fought down the pang of jealousy that stabbed at her heart. That was an emotion she'd never experienced before and she wasn't sure she liked it. Besides, she had no right to be jealous of anyone. The man was single. He didn't belong to her.

Zebulon took the basket and secured it to the back of his machine with a bungee cord. "I don't think Brittany will mind if we borrow *Pinkster* as she calls it."

Brittany's? That made her feel more at ease, but why it should bother her in the first place, she didn't know. Unless, she liked him even more than she thought, and she thought she liked him... a lot.

"Pinkster sounds like something Brittany would name something. I'm surprised it doesn't have a picture of a hippo on it as much as she says she likes them."

"Don't be fooled, you haven't seen the front fender."

"Oh, really?"

"Yeah, get on and you'll see it."

She walked around to the side of the vehicle and climbed on. There it was, in all of its purple glory, a smiling hippopotamus. "Well, I guess so. Can hardly miss it." One thing she didn't miss for sure was the way Zebulon's muscles moved beneath his clothing when he secured the cane fishing poles to her ride.

While he showed her how to operate her machine, she could hardly concentrate. He was so close the spicy scent of his aftershave was the only thing she could think about. She breathed a sigh of relief when he finally backed away and mounted his own four-wheeler.

"I guess we're off to my favorite fishin' hole."

CHAPTER FIFTEEN

Emily looked beautiful with the wind blowing her long, dark hair. The early afternoon sun brought out the natural red highlights. Zeb longed to run his fingers through the silky strands. At that moment she looked as if she didn't have a care in the world and her laughter rang through the air. "Are you havin' fun?"

"Yes!"

She hit a bump and her nice looking backside lifted off the seat. He laughed when the machine hit the ground and she bounced back into place. She was enjoying herself and he was pleased he was part of her delight.

"Wooohoooo! This is a blast!"

"See that cluster of trees over there? That's where we're going."

He loved the natural countryside of his land, and

where they were going fishing was his favorite place on the property. All kinds of foliage decorated the hillside, and trees surrounded the medium sized pond he kept stocked with fish. It was always a comfortable temperature inside the secluded, very shaded area, and a small, sandy beach-like shore marked the pond's edges.

He led the way to the easiest access point to the pond then slowed to a stop so Emily could take in the beauty of the area. He looked over at her and studied her while she soaked in the open expanse of the pool. Damn, she was beautiful. Would he be wise or a fool to open his heart and let this woman inside? He was afraid it was too late to ask that question. It was clear it had already been answered. Jasmine was gone and he felt the pain of the past fading away, peace was making its way back.

"This is my little hideaway. Look over there." He pointed to a small log cabin.

She raised an eyebrow. "Another outhouse, like the one in the yard at the ranch?"

"The one in the yard is not an outhouse. It's a tool shed built to look like an outhouse. And *that,* over there, is a fishing cabin. Have you ever seen an outhouse with a second floor?"

Glancing at him she replied, "No, but then I can't say I've ever really seen a true outhouse. And I was just kidding about that part. It looks like a regular little log cabin from the old days."

"Me and Granddad M spent many hours building that little fishing lodge. I was just a kid when we started, then after he passed, Bob and I finished it." He loved that little cabin. It had been his lifesaver after the accident. "It's got a fireplace and everything. Well, no air conditioner, but we didn't think one was needed because of all the shade trees."

"It's really beautiful. I'd like to see inside."

"Okay, but first we fish." It had been a long while since he'd taken the time to fish, and today he knew he shouldn't be here, he should be investigating who was stalking Emily. However, Andy was on the case as well, and he had a head start with all of the heavy stuff with the department. Her story was compelling and maybe would lead to more clues. Was he trying to convince himself that's why he was here with her? He knew the real reason. Today, he was going to relax and get to know this woman better. "I'll race you to the cabin!" He opened the throttle and took off, hearing laughter behind him.

"You're a wild man!" Emily couldn't stop laughing. All of the tossing and bouncing on this thing was going to make her ache later, but now she was having too good of a time to care. She followed Zebulon, who'd given up his cowboy hat for a ball cap. The Texas State Trooper department logo adorned the front and he looked sexy as hell in it.

The small house in the distance was right in front of her and looked like something she would see in a log cabin magazine. Rustic logs lined the outer walls. A small wooden porch was attached to the front with firewood stacked neatly against one side.

When they got closer she saw the little dock that protruded into the pond. A flat bottomed boat floated beside it. She loved the picture-perfect scene. She could see why this would be this man's hideaway.

She pulled to a stop beside him, turned off the four-wheeler and sat there for a moment taking everything in. The vibration of the motor still riveted through her body, or was it the thought of being here with him… alone… in this serene setting? She jumped at the sound of his deep voice.

"Honey, are you going to sit there all day gawking at everything? Or are you going to help me carry some of this stuff to the dock?"

"Are we going out in the boat?"

"I was thinking about it."

"I've never been in a boat before." Why did thoughts of Venice pop into her head? Visions of gliding through the waters in a gondola with Zebulon's arm wrapped around her played in her mind. Then her thoughts were pulled back to the present.

"You have led a hell of a sheltered life, haven't you? For all the heartache you've been through, you haven't had any fun."

"I've had fun." She thought about her life and realized she'd had happy and fun times with Randle, and many with Aunt Ruby, but nothing had been adventurous.

"If you say so." He held a pole out to her. "Here, grab this pole and that tackle box. You're about to ride in a boat."

Was her heart ever going to slow down? Excitement coursed through her when Zeb stepped down into the boat. Two bench seats were in the bottom with space underneath them. A small motor dressed the rear of the craft with oars lying against the sides.

"Would you hand me that stuff?"

She turned and picked up the fishing equipment he'd put down on the dock. Their hands brushed when she gave him the two cane poles. A shot of electricity coursed through her from the touch, and when she met his gaze she saw the spark flicker in his eyes. So he had felt it too? Sure not to touch him while she handed him the other things, she couldn't avoid laying her hand in his when he offered to help her in the boat.

"Just step in, I've got you, you won't fall."

If he only knew how much she'd already fallen, he would have used another choice of words. "And I'm supposed to trust you, just like that?" He pushed his cap back, allowing her to see his clear blue eyes, then held his arms out to the sides and stepped back in all of his damned, cowboy handsomeness.

"If you want to try it by yourself, go ahead, but if my butt ends up in the water because you wouldn't trust me, you're going to be sorry."

"Is that a threat?" There was that mischievous glint in his eye again. This man was making her understand it wasn't fear she had for cowboys, but it was the dislike she carried in her heart for her uncle that made her distrust them. However, she was beginning to recognize the fact she *could* trust, Zebulon.

"Try me."

His ear to ear grin sent the butterflies in her

stomach into flight again. "Mmmm, maybe I'll take you up on that challenge on solid ground, but not in the water." She had never felt as safe as when she took his hands. He guided her gently into the floating craft and her breath caught in her throat when they stood face to face.

A second was all it took for his arms to give her a steadying embrace. She met his gaze. His eyes, the color of the sky reflecting in the calm surface of the pond, held desire.

"See, I told you to trust me."

She only wondered if she could trust him with her heart. It pounded wildly in her chest when he pulled her closer. One kiss, that's all she wanted. Just one. Then, as if he read her mind, his lips covered hers. She leaned into his embrace causing the boat to rock. The kiss ended as quickly as it began.

"Whoa! Don't move."

Move? How could she move? He was holding her so tight, trying to steady the boat, she could hardly breathe. Or was that from his closeness? Once the craft was stabilized he slowly let her go and helped her sit.

The boat rocked and so did Zeb's world—all from a simple kiss. "That was close." If she only knew how close he came to losing himself in her when they were together, she'd probably run. If she did, he hoped it would be into his arms.

"So this is what it's like being in a boat, huh?"

Her cheeks flushed and he questioned the true meaning behind her words. "Well, kind of, I have a much bigger boat down on Richland Chambers Lake. Maybe someday we'll go down there and get some real fishin' done. But for now..." he started the small trolling motor. "This ole flat bottom and the pond will have to do."

He stopped the boat in the middle of the pond and prepared to help her bait her hook. The light fragrance of cherry blossoms emanated from her hair. How was he going to resist this woman if they were under the same roof for very long? "Here you go."

"What's that?"

"Bait. You want to catch a fish, don't you?"

"What kind of bait?"

"Worms."

"You *are* kidding, aren't you?'

Holding back the laugh that tried to escape at the look on her face, he pulled the worm out of the container of dirt. "Nope. This is the fish that live in this pond's favorite thing to bite." He thrust it toward her. "Here."

"I am not touching that slimy thing."

Taking her hand, he placed the worm in her palm. "Contrary to popular opinion, worms are not slimy. Neither are fish, like you said earlier, nor are snakes." He watched her stiffen, sitting very still.

"You don't have snakes anywhere on this little thing, do you?"

"No snakes, just worms." He was pleased it didn't take her long to get the hang of fishing, and after she caught a few, she even seemed to like it. "Granddad M made these old cane poles. Now when we're on the big boat, we'll use regular poles."

"Tell me about your *big* boat."

"I have a twenty-one-foot cabin cruiser. It's big enough to sleep two." He'd like nothing more than to spend a week, alone, out on the water with this woman. Jasmine would never go on it. Would Emily? He hoped she would. Now he was thinking into the future, but he couldn't stop his fantasies about sweet Ms. Em.

"Oh, I see."

"It has all of the modern amenities."

"I'd like to see it someday." She met his gaze. "After all this other stuff is over with, of course."

Her words were music to his ears. She would like to see it. "Sure. That would be fun." He didn't want to change the subject, but it had to be done. He wanted to get this investigation over so they could get on with life. "Speaking of the other stuff, maybe we should finish the conversation we started earlier. You said you found your mother's body?" The twinkle in her eye dissipated somewhat and he was sorry he was the one who caused it by mentioning her past.

"Yes, I saw a bottle of whiskey on the floor and some pills were spilled on the table by the bed. I tried to wake her up, but she wouldn't move." Emily sat with her pole out of the water. "Momma taught me to dial 911 on the phone if I thought there was something wrong. I picked up the receiver and pushed the buttons. It didn't take long for the police and ambulance to get there. Soon after that Aunt Ruby came. I don't really remember if I told them to call her or what. Some of it's a blur. Not only because they asked me so many questions, but I had to try to understand my momma would never come home again. I was only five."

He watched her put a worm on her hook and drop it in the water. "I understand." What she said reminded him of Jasmine's accident. So much of that morning was, as Emily had said, a blur. The other parts he'd tried to push to the back of his memory.

"From what Aunt Ruby told me, Momma made her sign papers swearing she wouldn't give me any information about my dad, either."

"What about your uncle."

"He didn't know us before my father left, so he couldn't have known anything."

"Surely someone could come forward. Grandparents? Friends?"

"The only friends of my mom's I knew were her druggie friends. I have no idea now who they were except Jack and Lilly Nash. I think Mom's overdose scared them into getting straight. They had a little boy, Randle, about my age. Sometimes after I went to live with Aunt Ruby they'd bring him to see me.

"I went to their house too. He and I went to different elementary schools, but we went to the same high school. After I got my driver's license, Randle and I got close and ran around together."

"So, he was your boyfriend?"

She shook her head. "No. He wanted to have a relationship, but I didn't have those feelings for him. He respected that and conceded to staying just buddies. He was the closest thing to a best friend I had until I met Brittany."

"I see."

"Even though Randle's married now, he and I are still long distance friends. We talk on the phone about once a month. He's always seemed concerned about my well-being and gives me advice."

"His wife's okay with y'all talking?"

"She doesn't mind, they live in Seattle. As a matter of fact, he says we're a lot alike. She's a legal secretary. When I got the job with Kail, Cooper and Mills, he said she was awed, knowing the prestige of the firm."

"Have you heard from him lately?"

"Yes, we've been in touch. I've kept him informed about what's going on. He said if he could be here he would, but I don't expect him to come to my rescue. As a matter of fact, he's the one who suggested I call Aunt Ruby to come stay with me, but as you know, that's not possible."

"I'm sorry to hear those are the only folks you have." He didn't know what it was like not to have friends or family. His heart went out to her. She didn't know it, but he cared for her, too.

"I'm used to it."

He nodded and prompted her to continue. "Anything else?"

"My grandparents on Mom's side passed before I came along. Don't know about my dad's. Therefore I was dumped on Aunt Ruby's plate."

Realizing how lucky he was to know his parents and grandparents, he counted his blessings. "Do you think your aunt ever resented that fact?"

"I can honestly say no. We love each other and she raised me like I was her own."

That pleased him. "I think I'll talk to her. She might be able to give me some information."

"That would be great, but she's on a cruise and won't be back for another ten days."

"I hope to have this done within ten days. Then you can get back to your job and your life." That didn't sound like he wanted it to, and he guessed he'd just hurt her feelings. The quick glance she gave him had a question in it. Did she think he didn't want her around? That was far from the truth. "I didn't mea–"

"I know what you meant. It's okay, really."

The tone of her voice made it evident it was anything but okay. She thought he was like her father and uncle, someone who would cast her aside, but that wasn't the case. He wanted her in his life. He just wasn't sure he was ready. "I know what you think I meant, but…" Leaning toward her, he took her face in his hands and kissed the soft, luscious lips he'd been longing to put his mouth on since she'd gotten in the boat.

He thought she was going to protest, but in moments she relaxed and accepted his gesture. Slowly he pulled back and dropped his hands from her cheeks. She tasted sweet.

CHAPTER SIXTEEN

Damn the butterflies in her stomach. They raced to her heart and caused it to flutter. She forced her sporadic breathing back to normal but didn't open her eyes when Zebulon pulled away.

"Was that the kiss of someone who resents, or dislikes you?"

"No." Could it be true? Could he really be the one man she could trust with her heart? She felt it to the core, but could she trust herself to know?

"Hey, look at me, Em."

She usually didn't allow anyone to call her Em, but from him, it sounded wonderful. Almost endearing. How foolish she must have looked sitting there with her mouth open and her eyes closed. Why did she react this way to this man? She opened her eyes and saw him point to the water.

"I think you have a bite."

The bobber on the cane pole went under. Once, twice… finally, she gathered herself enough to do the things Zeb told her earlier about setting the hook, and she pulled the fish out of the water.

Zeb grabbed her line. "Hey, that's another nice crappie." He held the fish out. "Here you go."

"Oh, no, I said I'm not touching one of those things."

"Now wait a minute, you said you like to eat fish, right?"

"Yes." What was he up to? He had that stinking cute gleam in his eyes again.

"Then if you want to eat the ones you catch in the future, you have to learn how to take them off the hook. I've already showed you a couple of times, so now it's your turn. Here."

She winced when he thrust the ugly thing at her face. He was really going to make her do this. "Oh, all right. Never say I won't try something at least once." His instructions were clear and she de-hooked the fish without a problem, then it started to squirm and wiggle. She squealed and tossed it quickly back into the water. The man next to her steadied the boat and laughed at the same time. Glaring at him did little to stop her own laughter.

Between laughs, Zeb started the small boat motor. "See, that wasn't so hard, was it?"

Emily slapped her hands together as if swiping off dirt. "Not hard, but gross. I may never eat fish again, but speaking of eating, I'm getting a little hungry."

"That's why we're headed back to the dock. The

sun will sink behind the tree line shortly, so we should have our picnic before it gets too dark."

Lying on the blanket with him was the first thing she thought about, but her stomach growling brought the sandwiches she'd made to mind. "Sounds good to me."

"Me too, I'm starving."

"If it gets dark, how will we see our way back to the house?"

"Hey, these newfangled ATV's have headlights. Besides, I know this ranch like the back of my hand. I could get home blindfolded."

"Oh, I see." She thought about what she'd just said. "No pun intended." Zebulon's grin not only warmed her, but the way his smile carried to his eyes melted her heart.

She stayed seated while Zeb tied the small watercraft to the dock, got out then took the fishing gear from her. He held his hands out to her and she gladly took them. Getting drenched in the lake was the last thing she wanted to do. "Thanks."

"You're welcome. Anything for a damsel in distress."

"Who said I was in distress?" He pulled her up with little effort. She followed him to shore and grabbed the picnic basket while he got the blanket. He was so strong and full of life she wondered if there was anything he couldn't do.

He laughed and laid the blanket on the sand. "You can't fool me. I saw the look on your face when you stood up and the boat wobbled around. You were afraid you were going to fall in."

"I was not."

"You were too."

"Was not!"

"Were too!"

"Not!"

"Too!"

They sounded like a couple of children arguing on the playground. Her gaze met his and blue eyes shined with happiness. For that moment the sadness she'd seen on his face so many times was gone. She couldn't stop the laughter that bubbled up inside her and billowed out, as she plopped down on the cover. Maybe they were being childish, but she enjoyed it. "Okay, I give, maybe a little afraid."

"Mm-hum… that's what I thought." He sat on the blanket.

Emily watched him remove his cowboy boots and set them aside, then he took his ball cap off and ran his fingers through his hair. She wished her fingers could feel its softness. Thankful the picnic basket was between them, she took the food out and they began to eat.

"I'm glad I made the dogs stay at the house."

"Why?"

"Are you kidding? They'd be begging for food and I'm hungry.

"Back to matters at hand. I'd like to know the rest of your story. I intend to get on this case hard tomorrow."

"Where'd we leave off?" She took a drink of soda.

"When your mom passed."

"Oh, yeah. Well, of course, as I said, I went to live with Aunt Ruby and Able. He never put a hand on me but his torture was making me go with him to the place where he boarded his horses. He knew I was afraid of them, but he'd force me to ride. I would cry the whole time I was on one. *'If you were a boy, you wouldn't be such a sissy'* he'd say." Loath entered a black spot in her heart for the man.

"Then one day when I was about ten, he made me get on the biggest stud in the barn. I was so scared, but even though Abe never hit me, the fear that he might compelled me to do as he said. He could look so evil."

"I can see why you dislike cowboys and are afraid of horses. He was a cruel man."

Cruel wasn't the word she thought of. "Bastard is more like it." Zebulon smiled his understanding and she found herself getting more comfortable with him every moment. "But the worst part is that big boy threw me that day."

"Tell me exactly what happened."

She cleared her throat as the memories of that terrifying day rushed her mind. "We were on a gravel road and I was holding on for dear life, but the strength of that horse was no match for a frightened little girl."

"Were you riding alone?"

"Yes, and Uncle Abe wouldn't help me or take the reins. He said I had to do it all myself."

"What an ass!"

"Anyway, somehow the horse spooked and reared up then took off running. I let go and landed on the ground so hard it knocked me out."

Zeb's silence propelled her on. Finally, she was getting her feelings out in the open. "When I woke up, the man who owned the stable was carrying me somewhere. I continued to act like I was out because of the conversation that was going on between him and Able." Her memory took her back as she delivered the words of the past.

"You son of a bitch! I said put her down."

"No way, Abe, I'm taking her to the hospital. Can't you see she's really hurt?"

"She ain't hurt that bad."

"To hell she's not. I told you not to put her on that horse, but your stubborn ass wouldn't listen. I think her arm's broke and her poor little face is riddled with gravel. She's bleedin', Abe. I'm takin' 'er and you can kiss my ass."

"I heard a car door open. I hurt all over, especially my right arm. My head ached and I started to tremble. I said a silent prayer for God to let Mr. Mason win the argument, then he placed me in the seat. I barely cracked one eye open and realized I was in a pickup. Mr. Mason's pickup, but I closed my eyes back and leaned over. I couldn't keep the tears from coming. My arm hurt so bad. After he shut the door, I heard them shouting at each other outside.

"You'd better get her out of that truck, Mason. I swear, I'll call the cops and tell them you kidnapped her!"

"You just do that, but I suggest you call your wife first and have her meet me at the hospital. Then, get your livestock off my property. I ain't puttin' up with your bullshit anymore. You hear me? You've got twenty-four hours to clear out."

She shook her head. "The driver's side door

opened, the man got in and the engine roared to life. My heartbeat pounded in my head and face, my arm throbbed to the rhythm as did my knees and elbows. When I heard the door slam, I start to sob out loud.

"It's okay, girlie, we're gonna get you taken care of, don't you worry."

She thought back on the older man who was so gentle with her. "His voice was kind and I wasn't afraid to go to the hospital, but I was afraid of having to go back to Aunt Ruby's house where I knew Able would be."

"Was your arm broken?"

"Yes, and when we got to the hospital, Mr. Mason asked if I knew my aunt's phone number. When he got in touch with her, he found out Uncle Able hadn't even called her yet. They were both furious."

"What a sorry excuse for a human. What happened when you got home?"

"After they dug gravel out of the side of my face and from the rest of my body, they put my cast on, which was pink, so I thought it was cool. Then me and Aunt Ruby went to a motel. She had one of her friends come and stay with me while she went home and dealt with her husband."

"How'd that go?"

"She kicked his, as you said, sorry excuse for a human's ass out."

He nodded. "So he turned it around and blamed you for their marriage falling apart."

Taking her last sip of soda she swallowed then put the can back in the basket with the rest of the items. "Pretty much." A flash of light came from overhead, followed by a loud crack of thunder. The sky opened up a torrential rain.

"Damn, I didn't see that coming. Let's get inside." Zeb threw his ball cap on, grabbed his boots then scrambled to his feet and snatched up the picnic basket.

In seconds, she lifted the blanket off the ground and ran behind him to the covered porch of the small log cabin. She could only imagine what her face looked like with mascara trailing down her cheeks. When Zeb turned toward her and began to snigger she knew it must be bad, but she didn't care. He wasn't laughing at her, he was laughing with her. Cackles built up inside her only to spill out loud and plentiful. She hadn't laughed that hard in a long time, but the snorting between breaths caused her embarrassment. That made the situation even more hilarious.

"Weee... beetttter... go... *snort*... in." She tried to catch her breath and knew he was trying to do the same. "Oorr... or... *snort*," She took a deep breath and realized how serious things could get if she didn't get to a bathroom. "I-I'm going to pee... *snort*... my pants."

He lay on his stomach under the heavy foliage that concealed his presence. He wasn't that far from the pond, but he could not hear anything they were talking about. He did, however, see the brazen man grab his princess and kiss her. He looked way too proud, especially when he had no right to touch her, let alone press his lips against hers. This had to stop immediately. The man needed to be eliminated as quickly as possible.

His princess's behavior was not much better than the man's. He may have to get a hold of her and teach her a few lessons. He had never seen her act like this. There was no reason for this kind of behavior. She was his virgin princess, and that is exactly how it would stay. This clown who thought he was a cowboy deserved to be put down—completely down—never to get up again.

Yes, that was exactly what needed to happen. No man had the right to touch *his princess*. He had worshiped her for more years than he could count, and he was not about to call it quits yet. If anything, he would take her away and keep her for himself—safe and far away.

There were lots of places they could go where he could keep her for his own. He'd have to think about it and make plans. This was no time for mistakes, especially if he were to do harm to the cowboy. He would have to make careful plans for that as well. He'd done his homework to find out who he was, and he knew he had been a Texas Ranger once. So if he wanted to hurt the man, it would take planning and patience. He had the ability for both.

Rain came pouring down and his princess and the nasty cowboy both took off and ran into the cabin. He just lay where he was and watched. What would they do inside that small space? Only his imagination could tell their next move. Would the ass take her to bed and rape her? It would have to be rape because she would never give herself to him. No. She would never do that.

His big blunder was laying out her clothes. It gave him away and he couldn't afford those kinds of mistakes. He only wanted her to look beautiful, the way she always did. He liked that dress and wanted to see her in it. His bad. That would be his last slip. He would have her as his own, and that was that.

CHAPTER SEVENTEEN

God, she was beautiful. He loved the way she laughed. "We can't have you peeing your pants!" With some effort, Zeb reached into the front pocket of his wet jeans for the key to the door. "Let's just leave stuff out here for now. We're going to track enough water in ourselves. And if you pee the floor, that'll be even more."

"I'm going to pee the porch if you don't hurry."

"It's harder than you think getting your hand into wet jeans pockets." He finally got the key out and into the lock. Pushing the door open he moved out of the way. "The bathroom's the only door on the right." She rushed around him and slammed the small door behind her, but not before he saw her brown nipples peeking through her wet tank-top. "There's a towel on the shelf in there, too, if you want to dry off a bit." The bathroom door opened, and a clean towel came flying out, landing on the floor.

"Here."

"Mighty thoughtful of ya, ma'am."

He liked seeing her wet and loved the way her top clung to her curves. The tightening in his jeans caused him to realize if she came out, she may see more through his wet pants than he wanted her to. Staying on the porch, he put his boots down, then unzipped his jeans and stripped to his boxers, which weren't soaked like the rest of his clothes. His jeans would dry by morning if he hung them over one of the outdoor rocking chairs on the porch. That done, he stepped inside.

How had he missed the storm cloud anyway? That was a stupid question. He knew exactly why it had escaped his notice. His mind, eyes, heart and soul were totally engulfed in Emily Tipton. The way she talked, the way she looked and the way she smelled.

He'd never been captivated by a woman like he was with her. He loved Jasmine, but wondered now if he was *in* love with her. She'd never had the same effect on him Emily did. Lust was the only answer. Wasn't it? Surely he couldn't be in love. Could he?

He closed the door then opened the window shades. The rain continued and darkness veiled the lake. He turned, glanced around the small room then began to unbutton his soaked shirt. How many hours he'd spent here trying to forget the heartache of losing the woman he thought he was in love with. Now he was spending time here again, but not alone this time, and without heartache. Maybe even with a new love in his life.

After tossing his wet socks, which were full of sand, out the door onto the still dry porch, he hung his shirt on the coat rack. He knew he had one pair of jeans and two shirts in the upstairs drawer. "Hey, I've got some dry clothes you can put on."

"Okay."

"It'll take me a couple of minutes, but I'll get them for you." Visions of her standing naked in the bathroom ran through his mind. *You've got to stop thinking about that, man.*

"What?"

Damn, did he say that out loud? "I said my socks are full of sand."

"I don't doubt it."

He gathered the towel then climbed the ladder to the sleeping area realizing they may have to spend the night in the cabin. Thoughts ran through his mind of what might happen if they did. No, he wouldn't allow himself to take advantage of the circumstances no matter how much he might want to.

He quickly dried off, thankful he could still wear the boxers he'd put on that morning. There were none in the cabin and wearing jeans without underwear could be uncomfortable.

When he went to get the garments out of the small closet, he saw he had the pair of jeans and only one shirt. Well, it would have to do. He donned the denim pants and took the shirt off the hanger for her to wear. He assumed she was about five foot five. He was six foot three and stood almost a foot taller than her, so the shirt would surely cover her. He caught himself smiling at the thought of her shapely legs being exposed.

She had to be ready for dry clothes by now. Climbing down the ladder, shirt in hand, he heard Emily's sweet voice and his heart leaped in his chest when he thought of her mere feet away, naked.

"Hey, are you ever going to bring me something to wear?"

"On my way."

The first thing he did when he reached the bottom floor was step in a puddle of water. "Damnit." He should have thrown the towel down and cleaned up the mess. In only a couple of steps, he reached the bathroom and knocked on the door. "Here you go." Her beauty took his breath when she opened the door and stuck her head out. Damp tendrils of hair framed her face, now void of makeup allowing her natural beauty to surface.

"That? That's all you have? It's a... a..."

"Shirt. It's a long-tailed shirt. It'll cover everything."

"I sure hope so."

"I'll trade you this, for your clothes and your towel." He held the shirt a couple of feet in front of the doorway. He knew he was tantalizing her, but he couldn't help himself.

"What? You expect me to step out there?"

"Only if you want this." He saw something akin to horror on her face and couldn't tease her any longer. "I'm only kidding." He handed her the shirt. "I'll hang your clothes on the coat rack to dry, but I need another towel to wipe up the puddles of water on the floor."

"You're a brat."

That man really knew how to push her buttons. Emily closed the door and let the towel drop then shivered. Not because she was cold, but Zeb's shirt brushing against her breasts made her have goose flesh. She buttoned it and looked down. Satisfied that he was right and the material did cover everything essential, she opened the door and stepped out.

"Ewwww." She glanced at the floor and realized she'd stepped on one of the puddle's Zebulon had been talking about. With terrycloth in hand, she bent to mop it up then realized her backside was totally exposed. Even if it was only to the wall behind her, she felt her face flush, dropped the towel to the floor, put her foot on top of it and began to mop up the mess along the floor.

"Hey, you might make some guy a good house mouse someday."

"Not likely." Marriage was something she hadn't thought of in quite some time. She figured no man would ever want her. God knew her dad and uncle didn't, but now, she had budding hopes that maybe someday, someone would. She looked up at Zebulon and those damn butterflies started up again. His chest was broad and smooth, tanned skin beckoned for her to touch it. If a man could be perfectly built, he stood in front of her.

She was staring and she knew it, but he was so handsome. Forcing herself to avert her gaze, she peered out the window at the darkness. Lightning flashed and raindrops looked like diamonds against the brightness.

"Why would you say not likely? Just because you feel like two men in your life didn't want you doesn't mean there aren't other's that do."

He stepped toward her and his warmth penetrated the fabric covering her body, but she couldn't bring herself to look into his eyes. It was hard enough for her to breathe with him standing so close, surely he would steal her breath entirely if she looked into his eyes. She didn't know what to say. Was there a hidden meaning behind his words? He put his fingertips beneath her chin and she closed her eyes when he lifted her face in an attempt to make her look at him.

"Hey, Em."

"W-what?" Why were her breaths so shallow? She had to force herself to breathe and a strange ache burned inside her most sensitive area. She'd never felt it before, but it wasn't unpleasant. In fact, she rather liked it.

"Look at me."

"No." She didn't trust herself. He was too close and she longed to kiss him.

"You're tempting me, woman."

She was tempting *him*? The feelings that coursed through her body were alien. She'd never been in a man's arms like this, and she couldn't imagine the man being anyone but Zebulon. His lips were so close his breath was like a gentle breeze against them when he spoke. This was the first time she'd ever contemplated giving up her virginity. She'd sworn she'd keep it until she found love. *If* she found love. Was she in love? If this is how love felt, she liked it. "How."

He put one arm around her then pulled her close, and his desire pressed against her tummy. That was another first. In the short time she'd known Zebulon Cooper, she'd had a lot of firsts. This was by far the most stimulating. She opened her eyes and gazed into his, the heat of passion burned in their depths.

He dropped his hand and stepped back. "I'm sorry, that was inappropriate." He raked his fingers through his hair. "But being close to you has an effect on me, well... like... no other woman ever has."

She missed his warmth, his touch, his breath on her lips. Did he say like *no* other woman? Her blood raced through her veins and her pulse beat wildly. Zeb turned her world upside down. She didn't dare tell him he aroused her, too.

Could he be feeling the same things? Maybe love? Or lust? Did she even know the difference between the two? The hardness that pressed against her belly only moments ago was a definite clue he wanted her, and it excited her to her very core, but was that where his feelings stopped?

Did it matter? Besides Randle, Zeb was the first man in her life she knew that wanted her in any way. There was that word again, *first*. There had been a lot of first time emotions with Zebulon. His comment thrilled her, 'Like no other woman.' She smiled. "I think I'll take that as a compliment."

"That's exactly what it was."

The sexual tension in the room could be cut with a knife, more unfamiliar territory, but one she was enjoying. She suddenly felt empowered in some way. Then a thought occurred to her. What if they had to spend the night here? Alone in this tiny cabin. Images of making love to a man, no, to Zeb, for the first time made her quiver inside. Heat rose to her face and she feared he would notice the flush. She turned. "Well, let me finish cleaning this water up." She didn't want to dwell on what might happen, yet seeing his exposed chest made her wonder what her bare breasts would feel like pressed against his flesh.

"I'll get it."

She backed away and watched him wipe up the remainder of the water from the floor. When he bent to pick up the soaked cloth, the muscles in his back moved with sinewy grace. She tried to imagine what it would be like to feel his hard body over her. Imagine is all she could do since she'd by no means done it before. Would she give up her virginity if it came down to it? Love, if that's what it was, changed a lot of things in one's mind and heart.

He threw the towel out the door just as another crack of thunder boomed. "Looks like we may be here a while. I'll turn on the radio to see if we can get a weather report."

Anxiety from the thought of spending the night there, or pleasure, she wasn't sure she could handle, raced through her. Was she that willing to give herself to him? Someone she'd known for such a short while? Was she in love? His kiss was pure pleasure and his touch made her tingle, but she had to get her mind off the subject or she would be tempted to ask for his touch again. Damn the questions. Damn the man for doing this to her, but she liked it. *Stop!*

She finally took the time to study the little area and not Zeb's physique. She glanced around the all-purpose room. A galley kitchen marked one side while the other side held the couch, a makeshift coffee table, a chair and one end table with a lamp and a radio. Another stand up lamp stood in the corner. A ladder, by the front door near the bathroom, led to the upstairs. Small, but workable. "How big is this place?"

The sound of static penetrated the room while he turned the dial on the radio. "It's twelve by eighteen."

"It has everything you need, doesn't it?"

"Yep, and the sleeping loft is even bigger because it doesn't have the kitchen and the bathroom. It's just one big room up there."

The mention of the sleeping area sent a quiver up her spine. Surely they wouldn't have to stay there for the night. "That's nice." He turned the knob on the radio again and country music filled the small room. Lightning lite up the sky and rain fell even harder. She was shocked at the look on Zeb's face when he glanced out the window at the flash. The alarm in his voice frightened her.

"Get upstairs and don't come down until I tell you to." He put on his boots. "Go!"

Her heart pounded. What was wrong? She didn't have time to ask the question before Zeb was out the door and gone. Fear pressed against her ribs and made it hard to breathe. She rushed up the ladder to the loft, sat on the bed and pulled her knees to her chest. She couldn't stop the tremble. It made her teeth chatter. She had never been so frightened. What was going on?

She heard something downstairs. Or did she? The rumble of thunder masked the noise inside the cabin. Was someone down there?

CHAPTER EIGHTEEN

By the time Zeb got his wet boots on and ran after the man, he realized he'd left the cabin door open. The intruder could have doubled back and gone in where Emily was.

Damn! Damn! Damn! He stopped pursuit, rushed back to the small dwelling and went inside. "Emily?" No answer. "Emily, are you okay?"

"Zeb?"

Her voice was small and the quiver in it broke his heart "Yes, it's me."

"Oh, thank God!"

The lock clicked after he shut the cabin door and turned the bolt. "You can come down now." Her small feet took one rung at a time. It looked as if her legs would barely hold her up. When she reached the bottom, he took her in his arms. "Are you okay?"

"Now that you're back, yes." She looked up at him. "Why did you run out in the storm like that?"

Her shaking began to subside and he stepped away. Concern riddled her eyes. If he told her the truth, it would frighten her even more, but if he kept it from her it might put her in more danger. "Let me get out of these wet clothes and I'll explain."

Soaked to the bone again, but this time he wouldn't leave his boots outside. If there *was* someone out there and they stole his footwear, he'd never be able to catch the bastard barefoot. Instinct had told him to take the keys out of the four-wheelers earlier. He glanced at the table, they were still there.

He grabbed a towel then went upstairs to dress. Could the shadow of the man he'd seen in the lightning flash have been Emily's stalker? Maybe he was seeing things. Surely nobody would be so determined to get his prey he would take the chance of being out on a night like this.

Once he got back to the main floor of the cabin, he noticed the static on the radio still filled the air. He walked over, switched it off then sat on the couch beside Emily. She looked so vulnerable and he wanted to protect her. Her voice was steadier when she spoke.

"Zeb, what happened?"

He cleared his throat. How could he tell her what he thought he saw? He took her hand and figured he'd be up front with her. "Em, I saw the shadow of a man through the flash of lightning. Out of instinct I went after him. Then I realized I left you alone with no protection." He glanced down then back into her beautiful eyes, fear restricted her voice.

"What? You mean someone was here? What are we going to do? Zeb, earlier you said we'd be here for a while, so, do you think we'll be able to go back to the house when the storm is over?"

"Shhhhh, shhhhh. We're going to be okay. I have a gun and plenty of ammunition. No one is going to hurt you I promise."

"But–"

"Em, I promise." He smiled and tried to calm her even more. "I also promise this will be the last time I come to the cabin without the dogs, or at least one of them. If they'd been here, they would have warned us someone was close by."

"I'm frightened! What if–"

"We can, what if, all evening but I guarantee he won't be back. Now, let's think about something else. Besides, maybe I was just seeing things." Her words told him she knew that wasn't true.

"Do you think it could be him? The guy that got in my apartment?"

"I don't want to speculate. Let's forget it for now." He went to the cabinet where he kept a rifle for hunting and a handgun, checked to make sure they were loaded then set the rifle in the corner, put the pistol on the end table and once again turned on the radio. He hoped to lighten the mood and get her mind off what had transpired.

When he turned away from the radio, the look on Emily's face was one he didn't recognize. Worry, fright, wonder, maybe even expectation, he couldn't tell. What was going through her mind?

All he knew was they would have to stay here for the night. He wouldn't take the chance and put either of them in danger trying to go back to the house in the dark. This latest threat only made him want to hold her, keep her by his side where she would be safe. With the feelings flowing through him now he didn't know if he could keep his distance. She was such a temptation he was afraid he wouldn't be able to battle his need to protect her, much less his attraction to her.

He had to ask himself the question again. Was he ready for love? Lust was one thing, but love? Hell, he'd loved Jasmine enough to ask her to marry him, could he ever do it again? It was hard to believe it had been over a year since that life-changing day, but every minute spent with the beautiful woman in the room with him now gave him the courage to move on with his life, and each moment it grew stronger.

He'd lusted after women, and had his share of them do the same to him, but those feelings were purely sexual. Emily, on the other hand, pulled the strings of his heart and wound them into a knot, and he sensed the feelings were on end as well.

"Why are you looking at me like that? Do you know something I don't?"

He opened the trunk he used as the coffee table and reached inside. How could he answer that? He knew what she did to him and longed to show her what he'd like to do to her, but he wanted her to want him as much as he wanted her. "Sorry, I didn't mean to look at you in any certain way." He reached inside the chest and pulled out a deck of cards. "Want to play hearts." Hearts? She was already playing with his.

"Sure, but you didn't answer my question."

"I told you I didn't mean to look at you in—"

"No, do you think we're going to have to stay the night here?"

She sat beside him on the couch and that's all it took for him to feel the stirrings of want again. "Yes, we will. Even if it stops raining, with this much water, it'll be too muddy to try to ride back in the dark." He saw the rise of her breast when she inhaled deeply, then watched it fall as she exhaled. "Does that bother you?" Staying there all night didn't bother him, but she seemed scared.

"N-not really."

He put his fingertips under her sweet chin and forced her to look at him. "How come I don't believe you?" The way she licked her lips only drew his attention to them. The thunder and lightning had stopped and soft, soothing raindrops fell and soothed him, and hopefully her.

"Maybe because I've never had a sleepover, or slept with a man before."

"Never?" Was she saying she was a virgin? Could it be true? He didn't intend to make her sleep with him, and after what she'd just said there was no way he should consider making love with her. Although he couldn't say the thought wouldn't burn in the back of his mind all night.

"Never."

His heart swelled with admiration for this woman. Very few women could say that at her age. He knew that not sleeping with a man didn't mean she's never made love with someone, but if she hadn't, next to him was the most beautiful virgin he'd ever seen.

He vowed not to take that from her, not tonight, her emotions were too vulnerable. He wanted to put her mind at ease. "Who said we have to sleep together." He was surprised at the huskiness in his own voice. Man, she was so innocent, so pure, then he heard her speak just above a whisper.

"We don't?"

She wanted him, he knew that, but he also heard slight relief in her voice. Her eyes were so beautiful and her breathing shallow, making his torment to taste her sweet kiss unbearable. "No."

Unable to help himself, he leaned in and pressed his mouth to Emily's. Her lips were too delicious to let the opportunity pass. The quiet moan that escaped her was not one of protest so he moved closer, wrapped his arms around her small waist, and pulled her to him. She tensed for only a moment, but why?

Was it from the anticipation of losing her virtue? Did she think he would force himself on her? Didn't she know he'd try to protect her with his life? There were so many questions.

That brief moment of tension slowly brought him to the realization of what he was doing. She was his client, he was supposed to keep her from predators, however, at that moment it would be him. *Cool down, you have to cool down.*

The last thing he wanted to do was stop kissing her, but he needed to know what was in her thoughts, the true reason she tensed in his embrace moments earlier. He allowed his lips to leave hers and slightly backed away. "Is something wrong?"

She slowly opened her lids and he wanted her to close them again so he could kiss each one, then her nose, her lips, her breasts, then lower. *Stop!* He warned himself.

"Everything's wrong."

What had she meant by that? She hadn't pulled away from him, so what could be so wrong? "Tell me, Em. I need to…"

"To what?"

Now her voice was throaty with passion and he wanted her more than ever. "Keep things right? I don't want anything to be wrong." What was *wrong* with him? Everything about this woman seemed right. Everything.

"Everything *is* right."

Now she was confusing him and he was mixed up enough on his own. He felt her seeking his lips, but he had to know what was bothering her, more than that, he had to keep his desire from overpowering him 'til he couldn't stop himself from taking advantage of Emily. One of his favorite songs came on the radio. "Want to dance?"

"I don't know how."

"Just let me hold you, I'm sure you will follow my lead."

Emily melted into his embrace when he pulled her to her feet. Safety and security flowed through his arms and filled her while they stealthily swayed from side to side to the soft slow music. This man was playing with every emotion she had, and his touch alerted every sensation in her body. His hold on her loosened and she met his gaze.

"See, you're a natural."

It amazed her at how she fell into step with him. She'd tried to dance before but it had never felt right. Now, with Zebulon, she could dance all night and never tire of it. "Well, I wouldn't say that, but I'm enjoying it."

"Me, too. Em?"

"Yes." She reveled in the sexy way he called her Em. She laid her head on his chest and the vibration when he spoke tickled her ear.

"Why did you tense a minute ago? When I pulled you close on the couch."

He was going to make her say it. She thought he'd get it when she told him she'd never slept with a man, but now, she wasn't sure. "Tense?"

"You can't fool me, girl. Something went through your mind for only a moment. I felt it ever so slightly."

When he paused from dancing, she tried to keep the steps going, but he didn't follow her lead. His hands were warm on her cheeks when he placed them there and tilted her head upward. His eyes were filled with concern.

"Talk to me, Emily."

The same panic she'd felt earlier swept through her. She couldn't call it panic. It was more like being anxious about what the night could bring. She had to remember she was saving herself for the man she loved, but these feelings were too hard to hide. She could easily surrender to Zebulon, but no, she wouldn't.

"I-I told you, I've never, well, I've never… slept with a man before." He let go of her face and took hold of her hands. When he stepped back she instantly missed his warmth. His smile was sincere and at the moment, she would give herself to him, no questions asked.

"You mean you're a virgin?"

Oh, God, he said it. He actually said the word she'd been trying to avoid. She looked down at the floor, unable to look at him. "Yes. I've been waiting–" He dropped one hand and led her to the couch with the other. She followed him without protest. Where else could she go?

Zeb sat beside Emily. "Look at me, please."

She forced herself to meet his gaze. His eyes were so beautiful and she saw nothing but kindness in them. "I know, a twenty-four-year-old… virgin, right?" Now he knew no one had ever wanted her. She was undesirable to all men. That wasn't true and she knew it. Men had tried to get her into bed in the past. It wasn't *her*, not the real Emily they wanted, it was her body, but she had no aspiration to be with them. Zebulon was another story, but he probably thought she was weird for never 'doing it' before, as Brittany would put it.

"Emily Tipton, you listen to me. Being a virgin is nothing to be ashamed of, and everything to be proud of. I admire you for staying true to yourself, and to a man who someday will be very lucky to have a woman like you."

His words restored some of her self-confidence. He didn't think her repulsive because she hadn't had a man, or old fashioned for saving her virginity.

"Really?"

"Really." He kissed her on the nose.

"See this couch right here?"

Patting the cushion beside her, she asked, "The one we're sitting on?"

"Yes, ma'am."

The tension of the conversation began to wane away. "Mmm-hmm."

"It makes out into a bed. I'll sleep down here tonight, you can have the loft. I'd never do anything to hurt you. You know that, don't you?"

"I know, and I appreciate it."

Zebulon grabbed the deck of cards. "Now, how about that game of hearts?"

She was almost sad to know she wouldn't sleep in Zebulon's arms tonight, but at the same time, she was happy. She knew she could trust him to do the right thing, even if she didn't trust herself. She watched the tall, strong, handsome and very sexy man deal the hand. He was wonderful. Brittany was right, he was a keeper. Cowboy or not.

CHAPTER NINETEEN

Zebulon fixed a pot of coffee in the small kitchen of the cabin. Sunlight streamed through the window bringing a beautiful day. Too bad he hadn't gotten any sleep. After he held Emily in his arms, kissed her sweet lips then watched her disappear into the loft in his shirt, his imagination went wild. The stirring in his loins at the thought drove him crazy.

The sound of dogs barking drew his attention and he welcomed the interruption. He went to the door, pulled it open and grabbed his shirt off the coat rack on the wall. Buck and Earl were outside, eagerly waiting to enter. "Oh, no you don't. You two have mud up to your knees. You'll have to wait out here."

Glancing around, he took in the situation. It would take a couple of hours for the ground to dry, but it already had a good start. He buttoned his shirt and reached for his socks. They were dry as were the jeans he wore yesterday. The chair rocked when he sat down and turned his socks inside out. "Look at all that sand, Buck." He shook them out and put them on. "Still gritty, but they'll have to do 'til we get back to the house." Both dogs barked like they knew what he was saying. Maybe they did.

Earl ran to the door. Zebulon thought if her tail wasn't attached, it would wag right off her bottom. He glanced up to see what the dog was so happy about. If he had a tail, he'd wag it too. "Mornin', sunshine." Emily's shapely legs went all the way from the ground to her hind end, and his shirt did everything to prove that. He could get used to waking up to her beauty every morning.

"Mornin'." She bent to pet Earlene behind the ears. "Morning, girl. Was that you that woke me up? You and the smell of fresh brewed coffee?" She looked at Zebulon. "Where would I find a cup?"

"In the cabinet above the coffee maker and your clothes are on the rack on the wall by the door. They're dry now." The last thing he wanted was for her to dress. He liked her just the way she was, but he wanted her to be comfortable.

"Thanks." She turned and went inside.

It was important for him to get back to the house as soon as possible to find out if Andy had any leads. The faster he could get this case solved, the closer he'd be to getting on with his life. Maybe a new beginning. Emily made him want to start over. Hopefully, she would feel the same way when the time came.

It wasn't love he had for the woman, or was it? Whatever it was, he liked it and wanted to pursue it when this was all over. He couldn't help but smile. A virgin. She wanted to wait and give everything of herself to the man she loved. The thought was pleasing. Maybe that man would be him.

~ ~ ~

Memories of their night at the cabin would play in her mind for a long time, but it was good to be back at the ranch house. Emily welcomed the warm bath water as she stepped into the tub then sank to her neck below the bubbles. She heard the faint sound of Zebulon's voice on the phone downstairs. The night before had been one she'd never forget. It would play in her mind a thousand times.

Zeb respected her enough to understand her feelings. He was amazing. It saddened her to think they could never be together. He could own her heart, but she would never be able to live on the ranch with him. Her fear of horses was one she could never overcome. It wouldn't be fair for her to ask Zeb to leave the life he loved so much.

Good grief, why was she even having such thoughts? She barely knew the man, but that didn't stop her from being... infatuated with him. If only he was a short, ugly, jerk, she could easily dislike him. But on the contrary, he was a tall, good looking, sexy as hell, nice guy. Damn him for making her feel this way!

"Emily?"

The deep sound of his voice came from the other

side of the bathroom door. He was in her room. "Yes?"

"Nice underwear."

She heard the enjoyment of his torment in his voice and swallowed the lump in her throat. Her bra and matching thong were lying on the bed for everyone to see. Her thoughts went back to her clothes laid out on her bed in the loft. Then, she was frightened, now, she just fought back embarrassment while she tried to keep her voice steady. "You like them?" Really? She just asked him that question? Her face grew warm and she was sure if he saw her at that moment he'd know what she was feeling inside.

"Yes, ma'am, I do."

She closed her eyes and forced her pulse to slow. The thoughts going through her head were inappropriate. She cleared her throat. "What do you want?" Amusement laced his sexy tone.

"If I told you, your cheeks would get red and you'd probably be embarrassed."

It was like he could see through the solid wood door. He could get under her skin faster than anybody. In more ways than one. "You're such a smart ass."

"Thanks. No, really, I'm going to leave in a few to go into town and get some work done. Do you need anything?"

"Not that I can think of but thank you anyway."

"Yes, ma'am. Isom isn't on the ranch today. I'd appreciate it if you'd keep all the doors locked and stay inside. Just as a precautionary measure. Would you do that for me, please?"

The reminder of Zeb thinking he saw a man's shadow through the lightning the night before came back to her. Surely he was mistaken, but he was the expert and he knew best. "Sure, not a problem."

"There's a .38 on top of the fridge if you need it. Do you know how to shoot?"

She swallowed the lump in her throat. He was serious! "N-not really."

"You probably won't need it, but if you do it has a laser on it. Once you grasp the butt, the laser will activate. If someone comes in you don't know, point it, aim for the red dot then pull the trigger."

Positive nothing like that would happen, she said. "Okay, okay! Now go away and let me enjoy my bath." His chuckle brought chills of warmth to her skin. She liked making him laugh.

"Will do. I'll be back about six. Don't shoot me."

"Go already."

The sound of boot heels clicking on the hardwood floor got fainter as he retreated. Then she heard him take the stairs and shut the front door. Alone for the first time in a few days, she relaxed back into the water and let her mind drift.

Even though she was by herself, she was safe. The dogs would let her know if anyone was on the property or at least near the house and that made her feel at ease. She went over the events at her apartment. Why would someone be stalking her? She didn't have any money, and her Aunt Ruby didn't have any money to speak of, so it couldn't be for ransom. Oh, well, she wasn't going to think about that. She wanted to enjoy her bath.

Startled awake by something, a noise? What was it? Realizing she must have dozed off in the water, she glanced at her fingertips. They looked like prunes. How long had she slept? She hurried out of the water, still not knowing why she woke so suddenly.

Her heart started to pound when she realized the dogs were barking in the distance. Was someone here? She grabbed a towel and dried off, wanting to get dressed as fast as she could. The barking persisted in the front yard while she pulled on her jeans then lifted a t-shirt over her head. She hoped she didn't have to get the gun. Afraid she would hyperventilate, she consciously slowed her breathing and approached the window.

Unable to stop the tremble in her hand, she reached for the curtain and gradually pulled it back. What she saw made her smile and she calmed immediately. The white vehicle with red and blue stripes pulled away from the mailbox. "Only the postman."

She put on her slippers and began to relax. One thing she knew for sure. It wasn't going to be easy staying at this house all day, alone, with nothing to do. She went into the next room where Zebulon's computer was and pushed the power button, hoping it wasn't password protected. All she wanted to do was check her email.

The phone sat on the desk. She picked it up and called the office hoping Brittany would answer and not the new girl. Jordan was sweet, but she wanted to talk to her new bestie.

"Kail, Cooper and Mills, how may I help you?"

"Brittany, it's Emily."

"Hey, how's it going?"

"Okay, I guess. How was your date last night?"

"Good, better yet, how was yours? I hear you had to spend the night in the fishing cabin... alone... with Zeb. Huh? Tell me, did anything fun happen?"

It would be useless to tell her about Zeb thinking he saw someone's shadow, her friend would only worry more so she'd leave that part out. "Oh, you wouldn't believe what all happened. It was wonderful, I beat him three out of five games of hearts."

"Hearts! That's not very exciting. Anything, well, you know, else happen?"

She wasn't going to tell Brittany about their dance, the kiss, the longing she had to be in Zeb's arms, either. That was her private business. "As a matter of fact, it did. I was in a boat for the first time, went fishing for the first time, got rained on and had to clean water off the floor. Other than that, the evening was uneventful."

"Dang, Zeb must be slipping. Oh, well, I guess it's none of my bees wax anyway. Did you just call to bug me or do you need something?"

"Who's working in my place?"

"Uncle David's, I mean Mr. Cooper's secretary is taking up the slack. Why?"

"I was hoping to do some work from here. Could you have her forward anything I can do online?" She glanced over at the printer/fax machine next to the desk. "Do you know if Zeb has fax?"

"Yes, he does."

"Do you know the number?"

"Yeah."

"Then she can fax me any paperwork I can do and I will fax it back for her."

"Okay, I'll tell her and give her the number. I'd better go, some other lines are ringing."

"Later."

"Bye."

Emily checked her personal email, and, as usual, had nothing, just a few in her spam folder. She was hoping her aunt would have internet access on the cruise and would keep her up to date on the fun she was having. It was sad she only kept up with Ruby and Randle on a regular basis and no one else. However, she didn't keep in touch with *them* via email either. She didn't even know why she had email. "Humph." She clicked off the internet.

Soon the fax machine beeped and she retrieved papers from the office. It was good to be doing something constructive. Engrossed in her work, she didn't realize the time had passed so quickly.

The dogs were in a happy frenzy and she heard the roar of Zebulon's pickup coming down the lane. She glanced up at the wall clock. "Six o'clock already?" He was home and she didn't have a thing fixed for supper. Why was she worried about that? It wasn't her place to cook for him. That was too much domesticated thinking. She'd have to be careful not to fall into that habit.

Butterflies flew like crazy in her stomach at the thought of seeing Zebulon. She was like a school girl. What was wrong with her? After checking her appearance in the mirror, she headed down to greet him at the back door and was almost knocked down when the mutts rushed in the doggie flap.

She heard his boots on the wooden deck and opened the door. He looked like someone's hero in a western romance novel. The most handsome man she'd ever seen. Damn those butterflies! Somehow, he made all her fear of cowboys seem like it had been a dream.

"Howdy. Hope you like pizza."

He bowed, and his smile threatened to steal her breath. She took the large box from his hands. "I love pizza." The aroma of pepperoni drifted through the air. "Mmmm, smells delish!" She went over and set the pizza on the counter then heard the door close. She turned toward him.

"You can eat now if you want." He took off his cowboy hat and hung it on a hat rack. "But I'm going to take a quick shower."

Watching him walk away, she noticed he moved with the poise of a lion. "That's okay. I'll put it in the oven and wait for you." For a brief moment, she wished she could shower with him. That would be a first, too. The thought caused pleasurable pain in her private area. A feeling she'd only begun to experience since she'd met this man.

"Okay, I won't be long." He shut his bedroom door behind him.

The clickity clack of Buck and Earl's nails on the kitchen floor caused her to stop daydreaming. "I know," she said and reached for their treat jar. "It smells good, doesn't it? You two are so excited, but I don't think pizza's on your diet. How about a dog cookie?" She smiled when they danced even livelier. First she handed Buck his then Earlene hers. They rushed out the dog door leaving her laughing and wondering why her aunt Ruby didn't like dogs.

CHAPTER TWENTY

He paced his living room floor for the hundredth time. He could see her loft out the window in front of him, but she hadn't been home in two days. His trip to the ranch to case the situation was bold, but he had to see what she was doing. Then the stupid storm had to come along. As quick as a lightning strike he was almost caught, but the cowboy chickened out of the chase and went back to the cabin. Coward.

He'd wracked his brain on what to do. And the decision was made, he had to go back. Somehow, he had to get her out of there.

How could his princess have gone with that miserable cowboy? He'd been having murderous thoughts about the man, he just wasn't sure how to act on them. He'd only murdered one other time and he rather enjoyed it. This time, if he did it, would be even better. This despicable excuse of a male had taken what was his. "Bastard!"

Emily belonged to him, no question about it. No man had the right to touch his princess except him. He would take great pleasure causing the man pain, and he planned to hurt him bad before... Some people never learned, but it didn't matter because the stupid detective was about to pay the ultimate price for laying hands on his princess.

It was going to take an elaborate plan, and he had to be careful and think it through completely. No way would he go to jail for doing what had to be done. He needed to decide where and how, the when would just happen. He would take his princess with him. She would know what he did, but he could never chance her telling anyone. Once she fell in love with him, he wouldn't have to worry about it.

He could not take a chance of this happening again. If she didn't *want* to love him, he would *make* her.

Oh, well, it didn't matter now. Soon cowboy would never touch anyone again—especially not *his* princess.

Zebulon let the warm water roll over his skin. The faint sound of Emily's laughter reached his ears. He liked the sound of it and loved the way she greeted him when he got home. He thought of her in his long-tailed shirt the night before and blood rushed to his groin. How could just the thought of her do this to him? He was tempted to reach down and relieve his ache himself, but he knew she was out there waiting on him and he wanted to see her.

He put on a pair of denim shorts and a white t-shirt with some flip flops. He wasn't planning on riding this evening, although he did have to go out to feed. He'd done it many times dressed this way.

When he opened his door, the aroma of the pizza he brought home had filtered through the house. He hadn't realized how hungry he was until that very moment. Entering the kitchen, he saw Emily pour a beer into a cold glass while another glass was already full and sitting on the eating bar.

"I hope you like beer with your pizza."

"Perfect." He picked up the glass on the table and took a long drink. "Ahhh, hit the spot." He couldn't keep his gaze to himself when she bent to take the pizza out of the oven. The roundness of her backside would surely fit perfectly in his hands. He forced himself to look away. It wasn't right to gawk at her, but it was hard not to. He was a man, after all.

Emily opened the pizza box on the counter. "How was your day? Any news?"

"Not really." He took a seat and put a piece of pizza on a paper towel. "We did find out something though. There are a *lot* of Able Collin's in this country. Over thirty in the Dallas area alone. Is he still living?"

"As far as I know. Once he left Aunt Ruby, we never heard from him again." Her heart skipped a beat. "You don't think he's here, do you?"

"Not sure, we're checking everywhere. How old would you say he is, and do you know his middle name?" A brief look of fear crossed Emily's features and he wanted to make her feel at ease. "Hey, relax. I don't think he's in Dallas, but wherever he is, I'm going to find him. Don't worry. Now, about how old would he be now?"

She nodded. "I'd say in his mid-fifties. He was starting to lose his hair then, so he may be bald now."

"What about his middle name." He took another bite.

"Richard. Able Richard Collins. Ick! I even dislike saying his name."

"Would you know him if you saw a current picture of him?"

"Oh, God, I hate to think about having to look at him."

He didn't want to put her through it, but it was necessary. "I know, darlin', but we need to know what he looks like and his whereabouts. The more information we have on him the easier it will be. When he met her gaze, he saw a little girl behind her eyes.

"It's been almost sixteen years, but I think I'd know him. I also know it's necessary, but that doesn't make it any easier."

"I'll be with you. When we finish eating, we'll go upstairs and get on the internet. Maybe we'll get lucky and find him."

Emily sat in front of the computer screen and typed Able's name into the search engine images tab. There were tons of different pictures that came up, but only one made her hold her breath and swallow the lump in her throat. His dark brown eyes stared back at her from a mug shot.

Her hand trembled when she pointed to the screen. "T-that's him, but it's not recent. That's what he looked like when I was little. Could this mean he's in jail?" Zebulon leaned in against her to get a better look and his warmth calmed her. She was safe at the moment, she had to remember that.

"Rough looking character, but it's just one mug shot and it doesn't mean he's in jail. Let's keep looking."

A shiver rushed through her body. The last thing she wanted was to search farther, but it had to be done. She continued to scroll photo after photo page. "Nothing. I'll get out of images and search the web."

"Before you do that, let's go back and download that mug shot."

She fought the urge to recoil when Abe Collins' face once again covered the computer screen. Zeb put his arm around her and she welcomed his touch.

"Are you okay?"

She wasn't great, but she was okay. "Yeah, I'll be fine. I'm glad you're here." She looked at him and eyes the color of the ocean gazed back at her. His concern was evident.

"I wouldn't be any place else."

How did he take her mind off of everything but him? She couldn't understand the feelings he caused in her, but she welcomed them at the same time. She cleared her throat. "Thank you." If she didn't get back to the task at hand, she was afraid she'd make a fool of herself and kiss him or something stupid like that. She focused on the computer screen once again. "I can't imagine Aunt Ruby ever being married to him. He doesn't look like her type at all. Ugh!"

"You never know who will be attracted to whom in this world."

He was right. She would have sworn giant ants would invade the earth before she was attracted to a cowboy or any man for that matter. Looking at Abe's face on the screen should have been a confirmation of that, but somehow, as a grown woman, she felt sorry for him and the mean and bitter feelings he held inside. He was probably sad and lonely, but that was something he'd brought on himself.

She saved the image to the computer, but Zeb hit print. She totally understood, but she'd never look at it. She went to the web search tab. On the second page she saw a headline that caught her attention. KERRVILLE NEWS: **Local Rancher Found Dead.** "What?"

"You find something?" Zeb pulled a chair next to her and sat down.

Her heart ran away with itself when she saw the image of a familiar cowboy on the article in front of her. "Yes, it's Abe, he's dead!"

"Dead?" Zeb put his arm around Emily, she was trembling. "It's okay." He handed her a tissue. "Go ahead and cry."

"I'm not crying because he's dead, I'm crying bec–"

"Shhhhh, I know. You never have to worry about him again." When she nodded he focused on the computer and read the words on the screen out loud. "The remains of a local rancher, reported missing three years ago, were found by hikers in the hill country around Hunt, Texas, about six weeks ago. Only today did the authorities release details of the identity of the man. Forensic dental tests confirmed yesterday the body is indeed that of Able Collins.

"Collins' death has been ruled a homicide. *'One execution style bullet wound was found in the back of his head,'* says Kerr County Medical Examiner. *'Other bone related indications show signs the man may have been beaten before he was shot.'*"

Emily swiped tears from her cheeks. "I don't think I want to hear any more."

"I understand." Zeb looked down and smiled when he saw Earlene standing by Emily's side, her head resting on the woman's knee. "I think Earl knows you're upset. Why don't y'all go take a walk or something while I finish reading this."

"I think I'd like that." She glanced down at the dog. "Come on, girl, let's get out of here."

Tail wagging, the Labrador followed her out. Zeb wasn't surprised Emily had captured Earl's heart so fast. His had been captured, too. Now wasn't the time to think about his heartstrings. He had to find out more about the murder of Collins and get to the bottom of who was stalking Emily Tipton.

CHAPTER TWENTY-ONE

Emily stood on the front porch of Zeb's little ranch. It was a beautiful place. The tension in her shoulders relaxed as she petted Earlene's head and listened to her soft pant. She could get used to living in the country, away from the hustle and bustle of the city. Commuting back and forth wouldn't be that bad.

Able Collins was no longer a threat to her or Aunt Ruby. That was such a relief. She wondered if Ruby knew about Abe's death or if she'd even heard he'd disappeared three years earlier. If she did, the woman never said anything to her about it. That would be a question she'd ask as soon as Ruby got home from her cruise.

"Hey–"

Her heart fell to her feet and she threw a right hook in the direction of the voice. The blow landed hard on his face. "Zeb! I'm so sorry. You scared the hell out of me. Don't do that again!"

He rubbed his jaw. "Don't worry, I won't."

She didn't know she could react that fast. "Are you okay?" When she met his gaze there was amusement in his eyes. She put her hands on her hips. He'd just scared her half to death and his reaction was one of entertainment? How dare he take her so lightly. "Does this seem funny to you?"

He laughed. "No, ma'am, not funny at all. You pack a doozy of a wallop!"

"Then why are you laughing?"

"Well, I-I guess because I've never been slugged by a woman. I'm a little embarrassed to have been taken off guard like that. I'm laughing at my own stupidity." He drew his hand from his face and placed his palms on her shoulders.

Zeb's eyes were tender and the look of concern made her want him to take her in his arms where she'd feel safe. But she wasn't safe. Her heart was in danger and so was her life, but only one was threatened by the man in front of her and it was getting harder to fight the feelings.

"Just so you know, I'm going to look further into Able's death tomorrow when I go to town." He dropped his arms and turned away from her. "I'd also like to get a key to your loft. I'm going to go in and check things out, look for anything out of the ordinary."

"Like what?"

"Bugs, point of entry, that kind of thing."

Another chill ran up her spine. "You think someone might have bugged my apartment? Oh, it gives me the creeps to think someone may have been listening to my conversations and everything I did."

"A bug isn't as bad as entering your place when you were home… or when you're not, for that matter. I'll check it out, though, and get to the bottom of this. Do you need to go there for anything?"

"It would be nice to have more clothes, and I left so fast, I forgot two very important things."

"What's that?"

"My cell phone charger and my laptop."

"Why didn't you tell me this morning when I asked if you needed anything?"

It would be impossible for her to give away the fantasies that went through her mind this morning when he'd caught her off guard, naked in the bathtub. "I couldn't very well have given you the key to the loft while I was in the tub, now could I?" She couldn't help but smile when his laughter filled the room. "What's so funny?"

"I guess you couldn't have, but I didn't think a girl these days would get more than two feet from her phone charger. It would be terrible if your cell went dead."

"You're a smart ass, you know that?"

"You've told me."

Then *she* had to laugh. "But you're right, that's usually the case with me, and my cell is dead. I don't know what happened. I guess I was just rattled enough I wasn't thinking. I put the charger on the entry table, but forgot to pick it up when we left." How could she think straight when she knew she was going to be staying in the same house with Zebulon, sleeping under the same roof as a cowboy, being around horses and all the things that frightened her?

She'd almost backed out of the arrangement, and if Mr. Mills hadn't insisted, she might have. However, staying in her loft was even more terrifying. No, she'd done the right thing. "Zebulon?" She watched him concentrate on the computer screen.

"Mm-hm?"

"How long do you think I'm going to have to stay here?"

That was the first time Zebulon had heard his given name pass through her lips and it sounded wonderful. He wished the answer to her question could be forever, but he wasn't sure he was ready for... forever. Nevertheless every day, everything about this woman brought him closer to finding love again. The feeling flowed through him like a lazy river making its way to the ocean. "I wish I could answer that. There's really no way of knowing, but I'll work as fast as I can to get this solved."

"Yeah, I know. What I don't understand is why can't I work? Being in the office surely wouldn't put me in any danger."

"What if someone wanted to kidnap you? What better place than in your work parking lot? What if you stopped by the store, not thinking? They could grab you and no one would know. If you had a flat tire, what could happen then? And on the country roads leading out here, well—" He couldn't wrap his mind around someone hurting this woman, but someone was out to do something to her, and it broke his heart. She'd been through enough in her lifetime.

"Okay, okay, I guess you're right, and I really do feel safe here. Plus, I had them fax me some work from the office today, so I won't be totally bored or feel useless."

"Good." She was so gorgeous when she smiled. He wanted nothing more than to kiss those lips of hers, but he couldn't. If he did, he might lose himself and become out of control. That was the last thing she needed.

He stood and immediately missed the warmth of her sitting beside him. "If you're going with me to your place tomorrow, I'd like to leave about nine in the morning. We can do what we need to, then I'll bring you back. Isom will be here all day, so you won't be on the property alone."

"I didn't feel alone today, either. The dogs even let me know when the postman was here."

He noticed Earl was lying at Emily's feet, while Buck was next to him. "Looks like you have a new friend."

Emily reached down and scratched Earlene's ears. "Yes, she's been quite good company, but so has Buck. When you're not here, that is."

Buck's tail wagged at the sound of his name. Zeb patted the dog's back. "Yeah, he's my little buddy all right." Moments of silence passed between them. It wasn't uncomfortable, just quiet and he realized he was stalling. He wanted to keep looking at

Emily, be with her and feel her presence.

Emily stood. "I guess it's about time to turn in. I need to get my beauty sleep. Nine o'clock comes early for a girl."

He knew her time to rise was usually much earlier. Kail, Cooper and Mills' doors opened at eight a.m., and she definitely couldn't get any more beautiful, so sleeping couldn't do much more for her. He started toward the door then turned back to face her. "I'll have breakfast ready at eight. Think you'll be beautified by then?"

"I'll try my best."

It was so hard for him to take the stairs down to his room, he forced every step. Knowing he would wake up and see Emily's face first thing in the morning was the one thing that made leaving her worthwhile.

~ ~ ~

"Here, let me do it."

Emily gladly handed Zebulon the key. She couldn't seem to hold steady enough to get it into the locks on the door. "Thanks." She swallowed hard and fought back the fear that rose inside her when the door swung open.

Zebulon took his cowboy hat off and tossed it on the floor in the hallway, then pulled his pistol out of the holster he wore on his belt. "Stay here, I'll be right back," he whispered.

She nodded and watched him enter the loft with the stealth of a predator about to pounce on its prey. Arms out, he held his weapon the way she'd seen police do on television, but never had she witnessed it in real life. He knew exactly what he was doing and it made her wonder again why he'd quit the rangers. Plus, he looked so damned sexy.

Hair in disarray, somewhat crouched and so focused, he was strong and she knew he'd protect her with his life. What that fact did to her heart was something she couldn't describe. He was the only man in her life who had ever cared about her in that way, but why? He barely knew her and he was willing to put his life on the line to keep her safe.

Mr. Mills seemed to care for her too, and she didn't understand that, either, but she welcomed it. At her age, it was going to take some getting used to, having men looking out for her after all this time.

"Okay, all clear, you can come in."

The professionalism in his voice reminded her of why he was keeping her safe. It was his job and she couldn't let her heart believe it was anything else. And Mr. Mills, she guessed his concern was because of all the money he had invested in her after giving her a job with the firm. Generic reasons, not really heartfelt ones, she'd have to remember that.

Zebulon joined her at the door and retrieved his hat. "You ready?"

Maybe this man didn't have feelings for her, and she was pushing back her growing affection for him. She still welcomed his protection but knew she'd have to keep in mind it was his job to keep her out of danger. She met his gaze when he put the cowboy hat on his head and he gave her a slight wink. His hand was warm when he placed it on the small of her back.

"All yours, you can go in now."

She glanced down at his lips and remembered what they felt like on hers, the sensations they caused. Ones she'd never experienced. Damn him for having this effect on her. There went the butterflies, invading her insides. Flutter, flutter, flutter. She tore her gaze from his. "Go away!"

He dropped his arm from her waist "Pardon me?"

Was she losing her mind? Talking out loud to invisible insects that insisted on assaulting her heart almost every time she was close to Zebulon Cooper? She swished her hand back and forth in front of her face. "That fly, didn't you see it?" That was the dumbest thing to say, but it was all she could think of. She stepped away from him and into her loft, needing to put some space between them before she made herself look even more like an idiot.

"Fly? I think you've gone bonkers."

So did she, but she couldn't admit it. She glanced back at him and gave him her most innocent smile. "Okay, maybe I was seeing things, but close the door before it comes inside, just in case."

Zebulon shook his head and stepped through the doorway. "Yes, ma'am." He closed the door behind him.

Facing the inside of the loft for the first time in days, she stopped where she stood. Her feet wouldn't budge to go further into the room and her heart all but stopped beating. "What the hell?" Her gaze traced every inch of the living area. It couldn't be, had her Aunt Ruby been there? No that was impossible, but what she saw had every indication that she had.

"What's wrong?"

"Someone's been here. M-my, t-he…" Bile rose in her throat and she forced it down. Who was doing this? Why?

"What is it?"

CHAPTER TWENTY-TWO

*Z*ebulon could tell something was terribly wrong with Emily and it tore at his heart. He stepped around her, turned to meet her gaze and put his hands on her shoulders. "Look at me, sweetheart." He lifted her chin with his finger and made her meet his gaze. "Damn, you're as white as a sheet. Tell me what's going on. How do you know someone's been here?"

She was fighting to catch her breath and all he wanted to do was pull her into his arms and make everything all right, but that wouldn't work. Nothing was going to be okay until he got to the bottom of this. "Want to sit down?"

"No." She looked around the room. "No, I'm just thankful you're here."

He could tell she was beginning to calm some. "Are you ready to tell me what made you react like that, and how you know someone's been inside your apartment?"

"Everything's perfect. Immaculate. My aunt started keeping her house this way when I was in college. When I lived with her, I called her, Miss Mighty Tidy, well, not to her face. I didn't want to hurt her feelings."

"I thought you said she is on a cruise right now." The blank look on her face told him she was deep in thought. She nodded and continued to stare at their surroundings.

Emily turned and started into the kitchen. "I want to check something." She walked to a cabinet.

Zebulon followed close behind and heard her gasp when she opened the door. She went to the next set of doors and opened them. Everything was in perfect order. Then he saw the tremble of her hand when she opened a drawer. He caught her when she stumbled backward.

"I think I'm going to be sick."

There was nothing he could do but turn the water on when she bent over the sink and threw up. He held her hair back with one hand. When he realized her knees were about to buckle he steadied her with the other hand. "Hang in there, Em. I'm right here. It's going to be okay, I promise." That was one promise he vowed to keep. When she was able, she was going to have to tell him what caused this reaction.

She was still shaky when she stopped puking. He let go of her hair, grabbed some paper towels and wet them with cold water. "Here, wash your face then let's get the things you need and get out of here. I'll come back by myself and look around later. You can tell me all about it when we get in the truck."

Emily welcomed the wet, cool feeling on her face. She was embarrassed all the way down to her toes, but she couldn't stop the bile that pushed its way out of her body. Standing to her full height, she wiped her face one more time, rinsed the sink out then bent to get the bleach from under the cabinet. "Of course, needless to say, this whole place has been turned into perfection."

"Want me to do that?" Zebulon pointed to the disinfectant.

"No, thanks. You had to watch me puke, the least I can do is clean and sanitize."

"Okay. Will you be okay while I take a tour of the place?"

"I'll be fine. Go ahead. I'm going to finish here, go brush my teeth, then after I grab my stuff, I'll be ready to go." She wasn't sure she was going to be fine at all and as Zebulon walked out of the room, the temptation to run after him and beg him to take her in his arms almost overtook logic.

Alone in the kitchen, on wobbly legs she made herself close every drawer and cabinet door then slowly walk back into the living room. The shiver that ran up her spine wasn't from a cool breeze. She fought the bile that once again rose in her throat. Even though she knew Zebulon was close by, she couldn't shake the unsettling feeling of being observed. Eyes, she felt eyes watching her and wondered if it was only her imagination.

It had to be, Zebulon would have found anyone that might have been in the loft on his initial walkthrough. Wouldn't he? "Zeb?"

"In the bathroom."

As fast as she could carry her weakened self, she made her way into her bedroom where the sensation of scrutiny subsided. She welcomed the reprieve and realized she was being oversensitive. No one was watching her. She and Zeb were alone and that was all there was to it. She wasn't even going to tell him about her silly feelings. He probably already thought she was a freak. Hell, she puked right in front of him. "Ugh!"

Zebulon walked out of the master bathroom. "What?"

Why, all of a sudden, was she thinking out loud? She was going to have to watch herself, that was one habit she didn't want to get into. "Nothing, just trying to figure out what to take." She hoped he bought that excuse and breathed a sigh of relief when he didn't pursue it but reached to unplug her laptop instead. "Thanks, my cell charger is right there, too. At least it was the last time I saw it."

"Yeah, it's here. Hey, can you show me how your clothes were placed on the bed before we leave?"

She opened the closet door and for a moment she couldn't move, only stare inside. "Look at this. Everything's categorized by color. Shirts on one rack, pants on the other." She took a step back. "I can tell you I didn't do this." If she didn't do it, and her aunt didn't do it, did it mean...? "Oh, my God!" She turned toward Zebulon. "Could whoever this is have followed me from my aunt's house? I-I mean, could he have been in Lubbock and followed me here?"

Her legs wouldn't hold her up any longer. She stumbled backward and sat hard on the bed. It couldn't be! Could it?

"What are you talking about?"

She had to gather her thoughts and fight the urge to throw up again. Swallowing hard, she forced the wretched bile down this time and tried to find her voice. It was impossible for her to speak at that moment. The shock was too much for her to take.

Zeb sat beside her, put his arms around her and rocked back and forth. "You know what. I think you've had enough for the day."

All she could do was nod. He was right, she didn't think she could take any more. Whoever was doing this to her may have been doing it for years! "I've gotta get out of here." Tears welled in her eyes when Zeb helped her stand and led her out of the room.

"I'll get your computer bag, I already put your phone charger in it." Before he let her go he paused a moment. "Are you okay to stand here by yourself?"

Her voice was weak even to her own ears. "Yes. Hurry." There it was again, the feeling of being watched. She hadn't been alone for five seconds before her head started to spin and a shiver ran its way all the way down to her toes. "Zeb, I-I –." The world went black.

~ ~ ~

Zeb saw movement from the passenger seat of his pickup. He glanced over to see Emily's eyes flutter open. "Em?" It looked as if she tried to focus. "Emily?" His gaze when back to the road then to her.

"What happened?"

He hated to hear her voice sound so small, helpless. "You fainted."

"Fainted?" She sat up and pulled at the safety belt across her chest. "How'd I get in the truck and get my seat belt on?"

"I carried you to the elevator then to the truck. I put you in the seat then strapped you in." He glanced over at her and his blood ran cold at the paleness of her skin. If he did anything, he vowed to get the person who was causing this. "What can I do for you?"

"Nothing, you did enough back there. I can't believe you had to carry me."

He turned his full attention back to the road. "Do you remember what happened?"

"Yes, I remember."

"Feel like telling me?" He saw her hand tremble. Pushing her wasn't his intention and he wanted her to know that. "If you don't, it can wait until you settle down some."

"I think I'd like that. Let's get back to the ranch. It'll feel better and much safer there."

Pride swelled inside him. She felt safe at the ranch, a place she didn't want to go to in the first place, much less stay at. Now she wanted to go. "Okay, Em, we'll go home."

Once Zeb pulled into his property, Emily knew she was safe. She couldn't believe a ranch had become her safe haven, but it had and she was glad to be there. The dogs greeted them and it was the first time she'd smiled since she woke up, but what happened at the loft still haunted her.

When she stepped out of the pickup she was pleased she'd gained her strength back. The thought of Zeb having to carry her to the truck embarrassed her to no end, but she was thankful for his strength and kindness. She didn't know what she'd do without him at this point, but when this was all over… she didn't want to think about that now. She wanted to get inside. Zeb's deep voice penetrated her thoughts.

"You need some help?"

"No, I think I'm okay now. I just want to lie down for a while." She wished he would lay with her and hold her, but the last thing she would do was ask.

"Okay, why don't you go upstairs and rest a while. I'm going to call Andy and see if he's found anything." He started to walk toward the kitchen.

She wanted to run to his side and stay there where she felt safe. "Zeb…" He turned to face her and her knees went weak under her. Could he be her knight in shining armor? The man of her dreams? So far he was, and she loved that. "Thank you."

He tilted his cowboy hat towards her, winked and smiled. "You're welcome. Anything for a damsel in distress."

The cowboy's sexy actions made butterflies

invade her heart once again. She smiled at the memory of their little boat episode. "Who said I was in distress?" While he walked away his laugh made her relax even more.

She heard the thump, thump, thump of dog paws and welcomed Earlene's company. "Hey, girl, want to go take a nap?" As if the Labrador understood what she said, Earl bound up the stairs and into the bedroom. "Well, I guess so."

It felt good to lie down and close her eyes. The morning's events had taken a toll on her nerves, but now it was time to get up and face reality. Zeb was in the office just outside her room. His concentration on the computer screen was evident and she didn't want to startle him. She cleared her throat to let him know she was there. "You look busy."

He swiveled his office chair around. "Well, hello, darlin'. Did you get some good rest?"

"Yes, I feel much better now."

"Good." He patted the ladder-backed chair beside him. "Come sit down."

She knew he had questions so she took the seat beside him. "I guess you want to know why I was so freaked out at the loft."

He nodded. "That might help me figure out some things."

She inhaled a deep breath through her nose and blew it out her mouth. "Okay, here we go." *You're safe now, you're safe now.* She repeated in her mind as the thoughts she had in the loft rushed in. "Once I started college, as I told you at the loft, I noticed

Aunt Ruby became more organized." She glanced up at him and noted the questioning look in his eyes. "In case you're wondering, I went to Texas Tech, so I could stay in Lubbock and continue to live with her, but it seemed she'd changed her cleaning habits. I didn't think much about it. That's why I secretly called her Miss Mighty Tidy."

"Okay." His brow furrowed. "Do you think Ruby has something to do with this?"

She shook her head. "No, I-I'm wondering now if she *was* the one doing the cleaning."

"What do you mean?"

"Well, there were a few times she thanked me for doing something in the house and..." She shrugged her shoulders. "I hadn't done anything."

"Things like what?"

"Well, one time she thanked me for rearranging the cabinets. I figured she'd done it, but at her age she may have forgotten, so I just said 'welcome' and let it go." She met Zeb's gaze. "They were arranged just like the cabinets in the loft were. Perfect. Every can in its proper spot, every piece of plastic ware stacked neatly on top of the lid that matched. It's crazy."

"So you think someone was getting into your aunt Ruby's house all those years and doing those things?"

"No, that would be impossible. I mean, how could someone pull that off and never get caught? None of this makes any sense." Her head was so crammed full of everything she couldn't think. Why was this happening? "Zeb, am I going crazy? When we were at the loft, I felt like someone was watching me, us. It was so real... like they knew our every move."

"You have a right to be paranoid. Someone is doing things that can't be explained."

"That's why I passed out. The feeling of being watched was so overwhelming, especially after seeing everything so perfectly in place. Then my closet! That was the straw that broke the camel's back." Tears welled in her eyes when she met Zeb's gaze. She welcomed his embrace and reveled in his warmth when he pulled her to him. Hot drops flowed down her cheeks and she didn't try to stop them.

"What about the closet, darlin'. Can you tell me?"

She nodded but didn't leave his arms. His reassurance was what she needed at that moment. "Just before I moved to Dallas, Aunt Ruby thanked me for color coding her closet. I didn't do it, Zeb. I didn't do it, but I couldn't bring myself to tell her I thought she might be losing it, so I just let it be. I'm so stupid for not mentioning it to her. She might be in danger, too!" The sobs wouldn't stop. All she could do was think of mistakes she'd made over the years by not confronting Aunt Ruby about some of the questions she'd had. "Who could it be?"

"Let's stop for now. Take a deep breath and try to relax."

She sniffed and attempted to pull away, but he pulled her closer and she didn't protest. "I'm getting your shirt wet."

"Hey, I've been caught out in a rainstorm, this ain't nothin'."

He had a way of making her smile even when she didn't feel like it. She snuggled deeper into his arms. It felt so right, so natural to be with him.

Minutes passed and her tears finally subsided. She backed out of his embrace and reached for a tissue from the box on the desk. "I'm okay now."

"Do you think you can go on?"

She wiped her face then blew her nose. "I think so." She tossed the used tissue in the trash.

"Is there anyone you can think of, especially an old boyfriend, who would have access to your house in Lubbock?"

"I don't have any old boyfriends."

"What about Randle?"

"I told you, he was never my boyfriend. We are just friends. Always have been and always will be. Besides, as I told you, he's in Seattle now and happily married."

"Any college classmates who seemed obsessed with you? Maybe a co-worker who tried to get you to go out? Anyone else it could be? A housekeeper maybe?"

"No one." She thought for a moment then realized she was wrong. "Wait, there is someone. Randle's parents had a key to Aunt Ruby's house many years ago."

"Why?"

"Aunt Ruby had a couple of cats and when we'd go out of town, Jack and Lilly would go check on them. Make sure they had food, water and clean litter boxes. Both cats are gone now and Auntie never got another one, so they gave her key back."

"Do you think either of them could have

anything to do with this?"

"Absolutely not. They are the sweetest couple, and besides, they live in Lubbock, not Dallas. How would either of them be able to pull such a thing off from that far away? No." She shook her head. "No."

"Okay, then. I'm going to put this visit on the back burner for now. If you think of anything else, I mean *anything*, tell me immediately."

"I will. I'm just glad Auntie is on that cruise because I know she's safe."

"Do you happen to know the name of the cruise line? I want to make sure she's on that boat."

She'd never thought her aunt may not have made it to her destination. Surely the woman was safe. "Do you think something might have happened to her?"

"I don't think so, but just to make sure, I'm going to check."

That made perfect sense. She'd be glad to know she was safe, too. "It's Carnival. The cruise left from Galveston and is a nine-day cruise to the Caribbean. I don't know the exact dates."

"It's okay. I'll figure it out. I'm an investigator, remember? Then I'll fill Andy in on the possibility your predator may have been doing this to you for a long time. Maybe he can do some research from the ranger database and see if there have been any similar cases in Lubbock. If this has been happening for years, this guy may be getting ready to make his move. That's why he was brazen enough to come inside the loft with you there and possibly visited the ranch the other night."

Her heart skipped a beat. "Now that frightens

me."

"It'll be okay. I promise we'll get to the bottom of this soon."

She hoped he was right.

CHAPTER TWENTY-THREE

I'm gonna go to the office for a bit. You okay here by yourself?" Zeb grabbed his briefcase and walked toward the back door.

Emily didn't want him to leave, but he needed to solve this case. "I think so. After my little rest, I'm much better. I just need to keep my mind off of... well, you know." The last thing she wanted to do was to dwell on what had happened that morning. "I think I'll boot up my laptop and do some work myself."

"Good idea. Keep the doors locked and your cell close.

"It needs to charge."

"If I need you, I'll try it first. If you don't answer, I'll call the landline."

"I'll answer, no worries. I don't have anything else to do."

"Okay. Isom went to get a load of hay but he'll be back in a couple of hours."

She loved that this cowboy had her best interest at heart and she was touched at his thoughtfulness. "Don't worry, I'll be fine." She reached down and petted Earlene's head. "Besides, my new friends will let me know if another porcupine comes along."

Zeb laughed. "Let's hope not."

As soon as he left, she missed him. Somehow it seemed he'd become her rock, but she'd have to get over that. As soon as this situation was resolved, she'd go back to her loft and he'd stay on the ranch. That was something *else* she didn't want to dwell on. "Dang, Earl, that cowboy master of yours has my emotions running wild!"

She picked up her laptop case and put it on the breakfast bar. "This looks like a good place for me to do my work today, girl. You and Buck can keep me company." She reached in the case and realized she'd never plugged her phone in. She needed to do that right away. It had been dead for over twenty-four hours. Hopefully, she hadn't missed a call from Aunt Ruby.

Phone on the charger, she went upstairs and got the papers faxed to her the day before. It was time to get down to business and get some stuff done. She welcomed the work. At least it got her mind off of other things.

Engrossed in her efforts she almost didn't notice the dogs barking. What were they up to? She glanced at her watch. "Oh my gosh!" An hour had passed since she opened her computer. Earl and

Buck were probably barking at Isom so she focused again on her computer screen.

Another minute or two went by and the dogs hadn't stopped their yapping. It was beginning to get on her nerves. "What the heck?" Surely if it was Isom they would have settled down by now. She stood and slowly made her way into the living room. When she slightly pulled back the curtain she couldn't believe her eyes. "Randle?"

Laughter bubbled out of her when she noticed the terrified look on his face. The dogs had him pinned on the hood of his car. She rushed to the door and went outside. "Earl! Buck! Stop, it's okay." She ran through the yard and approached Randle's car. "Buck, Earlene, enough!" She giggled with every step and wished she had her cell phone so she could get a picture of the scene in front of her. "Randle, what in the world are you doing here?"

He slid off the hood of the car. "Getting attacked by these mangy mutts."

At least she noted humor in his voice. "Earl, Buck, this is my friend Randle. Y'all be nice to him." The K9s finally settled down and wagged their tails when Randle bent to pet them.

"I thought you two were going to eat me alive."

"They were just alerting me someone was here." She gave him a hug. "It's good to see you. Let's go inside. I'm anxious to find out about this unexpected visit." She took his hand and led him into the house then into the kitchen.

"I'm sorry I showed up out of nowhere, but I've been trying to call you to let you know I'd be in town, and your phone kept going to voice mail."

Emily motioned to one of the stools at the breakfast bar. "Have a seat. Yeah, I left my charger at the loft so my phone went dead."

"Well that explains it, but I was worried sick. After everything that's been going on, all kinds of scenarios went through my mind."

"I'm so sorry I worried you."

"It's okay, Princess. I'm here now, everything will be all right."

Princess? It made her smile even if it did seem odd. What married man called another woman princess? But they'd been friends for so long, no point making an issue out of it now. She shook her head while she walked to the fridge. "Want something to drink?" She opened the door and grabbed a soda.

"No, thanks though."

"Sure." She took a seat next to him, opened her soda then put her hand over his. "Damn, sure is good to see you. Seems like forever. How's the wife?"

"She's well. Told me to tell you hi."

"That's so sweet. Maybe someday I'll get to meet her."

He nodded. "I hope so. Kailee's awesome."

"I'm sure she is if she captured *your* heart."

"Very funny, Princess."

"So, what brings you to Dallas? I thought you had something going on in Seattle you couldn't get away from."

"I was summoned here for a last minute meeting tomorrow morning on that Seattle project. I was going to call you to have lunch with me after the meeting, but when I couldn't get hold of you, I came a day early to make sure you're okay. I went by your loft first and when I got no answer, I thought I'd try this place."

She frowned. "How did you get this address?"

"Are you slipping? You called me when you were on your way here and gave it to me."

"Oh, that's right. I was so frazzled at that point I barely remember." She took a seat beside him. It felt good to have him here. "Well, I'm glad you're here. I want you to meet Zeb. I think you two will hit it off." She couldn't read the look on Randle's face but he didn't seem happy. "What's wrong?"

He smiled and placed his hand over Emily's. "Nothing. Nothing at all. I'm glad to be here, too, and I can't wait to meet your private investigator. Has he found out anything yet?"

"He has ruled out Uncle Abe. It seems he was murdered a few years ago."

"Murdered? That's terrible! Do they know who did it?"

"No, it's never been solved."

"I figured if something happened to him, someone would be happy about it. He was an awful man. The way he treated you was unforgivable." He met her gaze. "Are you happy he's dead?"

"Randle, why would you ask me a question like that? Of course I'm not *happy* he's dead. I *am* relieved to know he'll never bother me or Aunt Ruby again, though."

"I guess I should have phrased the question better. I'm sorry."

"No worries."

He sat back on the stool. "So tell me anything that's happened since the last time we talked."

Rather than tell him, she wanted to show him. "I'll do better than that, I'll show you if you want to take me to the loft. I was so upset this morning, I didn't get the extra clothes I need."

"You serious? I'd love to take you to the loft. Absolutely *love* to."

She noticed the pleased look on Randle's face and a huskiness in his voice. He must be happy she trusts him enough to go there with him. "I don't want to stay long, but I would like to get my things."

"Sounds good. Let's hit the road." He stood, took her by the hand and led her to the front door.

"Wait, I need to get my phone. Surely it has a little charge on it by now." She felt him tighten his grip on her hand.

"It's okay, let it fully charge. You know how batteries are. If you don't charge them all the way, they go bad. Besides, you can use mine if you want to."

He was right. It was probably only partially charged. "Okay, I probably won't need it. We'll be back before Zeb gets home anyway. Like I said, I don't want to stay long."

She followed him to the car then the drive to the loft didn't take long. Her heart raced and she swallowed hard. Could she do this? "Randle, I'm having second thoughts."

"It's okay, Princess, really. Once we get up there everything will be great. You'll see."

Fighting back anxiety, she stepped out of the elevator, handed Randle the key to the lock on the loft door and waited behind him while he opened it. "Would you hold my hand?" She welcomed his friendly warmth when he took hers and led the way into the apartment.

Randle glanced around the room. "Wow, this looks great! Immaculate as a matter of fact. I like it."

The loft looked just as it did that morning, but Emily refused to have the same reaction. Now anger and resentment seeped in. "Yeah, well, I don't!" She took her hand from Randle's, reached down and deliberately put the throw pillows on the couch in disarray.

"What did you do that for?"

"This... perfectness... is starting to irritate me! Whoever this freak is, his OCD manner is, needless to say, more than obsessive, it's manic, bipolar or just plain crazy! I don't know but now I'm pissed." She heard Randle suck in his breath and she met his gaze.

"That's a little harsh, isn't it?"

"Harsh? The creep is coming into my house, Randle." She started for the kitchen. "Come in here. I think whoever this is has been doing this organization for years. Even in Lubbock at Aunt Ruby's. I thought she was doing it, but now –" She opened a cabinet door. "Look, everything is in alphabetical order. Perfectly placed. It's just stupid to be this structured. Especially with stupid canned goods." Her anger got the best of her and she began to move the cans and put them in different places.

She was taken aback when Randle tightly grasped her hand to stop her. When she looked into his eyes she saw rage. What was wrong with him?

"Oh, Princess." He slammed the cabinet door. "After all I've done for you over the years and you treat me like this?"

Anger turned to fear. "You?" Her voice was barely above a whisper. "But how could you–" His voice was wicked when he finished her sentence.

"Be in two places at once?"

She couldn't speak. Her breaths were short and labored. How could she have been so blind? She nodded. His evil laughter chilled her to the bone.

"I wasn't, Princess. I could never leave you."

CHAPTER TWENTY-FOUR

"You're hunch was right, Zeb. Randle Nash is your guy."

"You've gotta be shittin' me, Andy!" Zeb swallowed the bile in his throat. Why had he let his gut feeling go so long without acting on it?

"Nope. The man has never been married, doesn't live in Seattle, his cell phone records say he's here in Dallas and has been since about the same time Emily Tipton moved here."

With each word, he slammed his hand on top of the desk. "Damn, damn, damn!"

"Before this, his cell pinged off of towers in Lubbock."

"Emily was right! He's been stalking her for years!" He had to do something and now. "I'm going to call her and warn her to be aware and not to contact him again. Hell, man, he knows where I live." He dialed her number.

"How does he know that?"

He couldn't believe this. "She told him. She thought he was her best friend and tells him just about everything she does." The phone purred from the other end then Emily's voicemail picked up. At the sound of the tone, he left a message praying she'd get it.

He dialed his house phone and received the same response. "Come on, Em, pick up!" His heart sank to his feet when there was no answer. "She's not at the ranch. I told her to stay by the phone and she said she would." Something was terribly wrong and his bet was Randle Nash was behind it.

"I'm going to the loft. Alert the police and the rangers for backup. If what you told me about the vent on the roof is correct, I'm going in." He was going to get this son of a bitch one way or the other.

Zeb took a right turn way too fast. He'd had a gut feeling all along, but Em had been so sure it wasn't Nash, he didn't want to upset her by pursuing it. He should have done it behind her back long before now. That's what happened when an investigator got soft. He made important mistakes that could cost her life.

He would do anything for her, yet he'd let her down. Damn! He'd never forgive himself. Randle Nash was off his rocker. What man in his right mind would color code a woman's clothes in her closet, put canned goods in alphabetical order or lay clothes out for her to wear then disappear without a trace? That was crazy all in itself. He was dealing with a very sick minded man that was completely obsessed with Emily and had been, probably, since they were children.

Being preoccupied with Emily was not hard for him to comprehend. He couldn't get her off his mind either, but following her for years, getting into her homes and everything else was crazy sick. If he looked this guy up in a psycho textbook he'd most likely fill every line perfectly. He turned another corner, finally on the right street. He was going to do this the Randle way.

He pulled into the parking lot, went into the building and got in the elevator. He by-passed Emily's floor and went to the roof. Andy told him how Randle got access and he was about to do the same. Something told him it was the way to go. Follow your gut, or so he'd always been told. Too bad he hadn't stuck to that instinct. He pushed all of that out of his mind and concentrated on his job and nothing else.

After a short walk in the direction of Emily's place, he saw the grid Andy had described. Every screw had been removed, no doubt by Nash, which made it move freely. Carefully he lifted it and slid it to the side. The metal vent that it covered was quite large and he eased inside with no problem, He pulled the cover back into place before he continued. The ridges inside the vent made it easy to go down slowly without falling. It took quite a while before the vent curved, and made its way to his destination.

He didn't open the vent grate into the loft because he heard voices and wanted to know what he was getting himself into. He was thankful his friends were on alert. All he had to do was press one button on his phone and half the Texas Rangers would swarm the place. They and the police department were probably circling the area now.

The voices below grew louder and he was able to see into the room through the grate slits. He couldn't believe she was standing there naked. What the hell was Nash making her do? Surely the man wasn't going to rape her. He'd kill him for that!

No, it wasn't rape. His heart slowed. She was getting dressed, thank God. When she put on a pair of pink underwear, he heard Randle chiding her and complimenting her at the same time. He decided to listen for a moment before he interrupted the scene. He trusted Emily, but not the crazy man with her. If she came into real danger he'd be there in a flash.

Randle reached for Emily's bra to fasten it, but she slapped his arm away. "Don't touch me."

"Oh, Princess, you don't know how many times I've dreamed of helping you do this."

"I don't care about your dreams, just stay away from me, Randle!"

"So that's how you want to play?" Randle shook his head. "This is not princess behavior you know. I want to treat you well, but I'll have to treat you completely different if you keep it up." His voice softened. "I won't be able to confide in you my deepest secret."

Zeb could only pray Emily would keep her cool. *Just play along with him, Em. Don't piss him off.*

"Now that you're fastened, straighten that strap

and put on the cute little dress I picked out for you to wear. The colors are perfect for you. I like it just as much now as I did the first time I tried to get you to wear it." He chuckled. "That little mistake is the one that almost cost me everything. But now we'll be together and I can finally see you in this." He held the dress up. "Oh, yes! I like it a lot." Randle looked into Emily's eyes. "Don't you?"

"Of course I do or I wouldn't have bought it."

"Well, I'm glad to hear that, Princess, because I'd really hate to demote you from that title. You know, I've done lots of things for you that you know nothing about."

"I'm well aware of closets and cupboards, what else is there?"

"Are you going to act like a good little princess for me?"

Come on, Em, just say yes. Appease the guy until he tells you everything. Zeb pressed the record button on his phone. He wanted to get every word. Nash's malicious smile made him sick to his stomach.

"For one thing there's good 'ole Uncle Abe." Randle reached out and stroked her hair. "I did enjoy making him suffer for what he'd done to you. He was a complete ass you know." He shook his head. "I wanted to torture him even longer but he pissed me off so bad that day I had to shoot him in the head. Of course he deserved it, but I wasn't done with the things that really made him hurt."

"You killed Abe? I can't believe it!"

"Believe it, Princess. Want to hear about it?"

"No!"

"Aren't you going to thank me for getting rid of your biggest problem? I did you a huge favor, ya know?"

"What about Kailee, your wife. How did you explain all this to her? It has to be strange for her."

"You are slow, Princess. There *is* no Kailee. I made her up to remove suspicion on your part. Otherwise, you might have guessed it was me taking care of you and sometimes your aunt. She was no neater than you were. But I found ways to keep things neat and tidy. I thought it funny when I realized the two of you assumed each other was doing the cleaning. It made my job of getting that house straightened up so much easier."

"Yeah, we're just a couple of slobs, I know. Sorry."

"Apology accepted. Just don't let it happen again." He took Emily by the arm. "Now let's go out on the balcony. I want to see that pretty little dress with sunbeams shining down on you."

Emily tried to free herself from his grasp. "You can let me go I'm not going to fight you, Randle."

"Oh, goodie, goodie, you're starting to see things my way. Maybe later I'll take your virginity slow and easy. By candlelight of course, Princess. I want you to enjoy every minute of my lovemaking."

Zeb's blood boiled at the man's words. All color rushed from Emily's face as Nash kept hold of her arm and led her through the sliding doors and on to the small deck. He heard the shock in her voice when the man confessed to Abe's murder. After being so called 'friends' with Randle, she probably couldn't believe he was capable of murder.

"Enough is enough," he stated.

Now was his chance. He opened the vent, climbed down the bookcase and made his way to the far corner of the room to wait for them to come back in. Randle was laughing when he stepped back inside. It was time to put an end to this nonsense.

"Hey, *asshole*, are you done torturing Emily?" He stepped out from his vantage point. "Because I say you are."

"Cowboy, how nice of you to join us. I'm glad you could be here to say goodbye to this beautiful young lady before I take her away."

"Oh, she's not going anywhere. You can take that to the bank."

"Who made you the banker?"

"I did." He wanted a piece of him like he'd never wanted from anyone before. This lunatic had done nothing but cause problems since Emily had known him and it was over as of now. He gave the crazy man the 'come on' sign with his fingers. "Come on, let's finish this." He crouched and got ready for an attack.

Randle reached in his pocket and pulled out a switchblade and engaged it. He waved it back and forth a few times. "Not so anxious now, cowboy?" He laughed. "You know my princess hates cowboys don't you?"

"Not this cowboy." Randle rushed at him with the knife and he easily knocked his strike away and got in a good right hook to Nash's jaw. When the man got up he rushed back at Zeb but the knife was gone. Randle grabbed him and wrestled him to the floor. The hair-brained guy was almost his size, but it was clear he had no experience in fighting.

He rolled back and forth with the idiot a few times, but it had already turned into a hugging match, especially when he could end it here and now. He pulled his right fist back then let it fly into the man's face. After a few more shots like that Randle Nash lay on the floor and didn't move. Out like a light.

Zeb quickly took out his handcuffs, turned the moron face down and cuffed him just in case he woke up. He then hit the button on his phone that called his buddies. He immediately rushed over to Emily, picked her up and carried her to the bed before she fell. He laid her down but refused to let go unless she asked. She was shaking so badly she might never get over this experience.

"Darlin', you all right?" Her head nodded against his chest. "It's over now. Totally over. You're safe. I promise. I'll never let anyone hurt you again, trust me."

Tears streamed freely down Emily's cheeks. She did trust him. With every part of her being, and she loved him more than words could say. But loving him could hurt her. He'd saved her from no telling what fate. She couldn't believe what had transpired in the last few hours. More than anything she wanted to wrap her arms tighter around him and hold on for dear life, but that was impossible.

The front door to the loft crashed open. A shout and more than one set of heavy footsteps entered the apartment.

"Police! Come out now with your hands up!"

Zeb released his embrace, gave her a sign to stay where she was, then stood. "The suspect is in there on the floor, handcuffed! I'm Zebulon Cooper, former Texas Ranger. Miss Tipton is okay."

When she saw a man dressed in a white shirt, black pants, a necktie and a cowboy hat step in the room, she saw the look of relief on Zeb's face. He greeted the man with a friendly handshake.

"Good to see ya, Jonathan."

"You, too, Cooper. Why the hell didn't you let us in on this case a little earlier? Andy ended up telling me about it only a couple of hours ago."

"Figured I could handle it."

Jonathan smiled. "And that you did. That guy out there has a mighty nice bruise formin' on his left cheek. And a couple of black eyes to boot."

Emily wiped tears from her face and stood. She remembered the altercation between the two men. It was clear Zeb had the upper hand from the beginning. She was only glad he showed up when he did. Imagining what might have happened sickened her.

Zeb put his arm around Emily's waist. "Ranger Jonathan, this is Emily Tipton."

The ranger tipped his hat toward her. "Ma'am." He glanced at Zeb. "You've got an awfully good man on your team here. Really good at what he does."

"Yes, I saw that first hand." Her nerves began to settle and true realization that all the turmoil in her life was over. She looked into Zeb's blue eyes. "Thank you, Zeb. I don't know what I would have done if you hadn't shown up."

"I'd do anything for you, Em."

She couldn't allow herself to fall deeper under his spell. Emily cleared her throat. "How did you know I was here?" It was the only thing she could think to say to stop those pesky bugs from flitting into the depths of her heart.

Mesmerized by the story Zebulon told about how Andy helped him investigate Randle she listened intently. How could she have been so stupid to believe Randle's lies? Just one more reason she couldn't trust *any* man. Earlier she thought she could trust Zeb with her life, but trusting him with her heart was not something she was willing to do.

None of this had anything to do with him living on a ranch and her fear of horses. However, she doubted her terror of the equines would ever get better. Nevertheless, her subconscious told her, with Zebulon's help, it would be easy to eventually trust him with her love, but her conscious mind wouldn't allow it.

CHAPTER TWENTY-FIVE

Emily glanced at the wall clock in her office. It was almost 5 o'clock and she couldn't wait to get home to her new apartment. Brittany wanted to take her out to eat for her birthday, but she feared a surprise party so she declined the invitation. The last thing she wanted to be reminded of was turning a quarter century old. However, life was almost back to normal after the events that turned her life upside down, but she vowed to be a trooper and so far she had been.

Trooper reminded her of Zeb. It had been a couple of weeks since she told him it wouldn't work out between them. Her heart broke when he walked away, but it had to be. She could never live on the ranch. Though she'd conquered her fear of cowboys, horses were a fright that reared its ugly head every time she even thought about them. She shivered in disgust.

The worst thing about not being with him every day was she missed the hell out of him, the dogs, even Isom! She didn't want to think about that now. Missing Zeb was the core of her sadness. She wanted to get home and unpack some more of her things and get her mind off of the man she loved but could never have.

The intercom on her desk squawked and Mr. Mill's voice interrupted the quiet in her office. What could he want this time of day on a Friday?

"Miss Tipton, could you please come to the conference room on the second floor?"

The conference room? She didn't know he had a meeting. "Yes, sir. I'll be right down."

"Good. If you want to bring your things, you can go home from here."

What the heck was going on? This was a strange request, but she'd do what she was asked. After all, it *was* her job.

She gathered her belongings, made her way to the elevator and pushed the second floor button. It was only seconds before the doors opened and she stepped out. It was dark, only one tiny light was on at the end of the hallway. The lights in the conference room were off so she knocked before she stepped inside. One step inside and the lights came on. The room was filled with people and she heard their voices in unison.

"Surprise!"

This was what she'd been trying to avoid by turning Brittany down. Now she was here so no matter how hard it was to put on a happy face, she would make it happen. Smiling she said, "What?" The big room was decorated with streamers, balloons and a birthday cake on a table.

Mr. Mills stepped up to her. "Happy 25th birthday, Emily."

"Why, Mr. Mills, thank you." Who told him it was her birthday? She looked at her boss. "How did you know–" A familiar voice interrupted her in mid-sentence. She turned and saw the person it belonged to. Although she didn't think it possible, joy filled her heart. "Auntie! What are you doing here?" She hugged Aunt Ruby with all her might.

"I wouldn't have missed your birthday party, dear. This is a very special day! Besides, you know how I am, someone had to be in charge."

"That figures." She gave Ruby one last squeeze then released her hug and met the woman's gaze. "How was your cruise? I want to hear all about it."

"We'll have time to catch up later. Right now, you have a party to attend." Ruby turned toward the crowd of people gathered and swept her arm around the area. "Look who all's here, dear."

The first person her gaze landed on stood there in all his handsomeness. Hat in hand with a sexy as hell sideways smile on his face. When he started toward her, she feared her knees would buckle. His smooth, deep voice made her want to melt into the safety of his arms.

"Em," he greeted.

"Cowboy."

"How ya doin'?"

Had the world disappeared and left them standing alone in their own little space? She knew there were many people around, but she could only focus on Zeb. She nodded and fought to catch her breath. "Great. You?"

"Besides missing seeing you on the ranch every day? Good."

"Well, you two." Aunt Ruby interrupted. "We need to move along, we have a lot of greeting to do and some big news to share!"

Centered on the people in the room once again, Emily cleared her throat and met Zeb's gaze. "Excuse me. I guess I'd better do what I'm told." He smiled and gave her a wink that made those thoughtless butterflies flutter in her heart threatening to make it stop beating.

"Maybe we'll talk later."

She wanted nothing more than to be in his company. "Maybe."

Ruby took Emily by the arm and led her to a sofa. "I want you to have a seat, dear."

"But shouldn't I greet the rest of the guests?"

"I think the music and the wine will keep them occupied for a while longer. There's something important you need to know."

There was a smile on Auntie's face and a glint in her eye. What was she up to? "Ooookay." She took a seat, as told, and noticed Mr. Mills, Brittany and Mrs. Mills approach. Mr. Mills sat next to her on one side and Aunt Ruby on the other, Brittany and Mrs. Mills sat across from them on another couch. She looked at her new best friend who seemed excited.

"Brittany, what's going on?"

"I can't wait for you to find out! I'm ecstatic

about the news. I think you will be, too. Aunt Ruby, tell her already."

She turned her attention to her aunt when she heard her voice.

Ruby cleared her throat. "I think we're going to make you a happy woman today, Emily Tipton."

"I'm happy with y'all just being here." She glanced at the people gathered around her. The folks she'd grown to love over the past few months. She felt Zebulon's presence standing behind her, then the warmth of his hand on her shoulder. She didn't shrug it off, instead, she welcomed it.

"No, I mean, well…" Ruby shrugged. "I'm just going to come right out and tell you. I've been keeping a secret from you for many years. It's weighed heavy on my heart, but I was legally sworn, as you know, by the papers your mother made me sign when you were little."

Her pulse quickened and she bit her lip. She struggled for a breath then another. Was this about her–? "Auntie is this something about my dad? Do you know who he is? Where he is?" It was her twenty-fifth birthday. Today was the day. Why hadn't she realized it until that very moment? Maybe because she feared the truth?

Now, at twenty-five years old. She wasn't sure she wanted to know about any of it. She'd come to terms with him not wanting her and the hurt was hidden deep inside. Maybe she should keep it there. "Never mind. I-I'm not sure I want to hear it." Ruby gave her a reassuring smile that instilled comfort.

"Oh, you want to hear it, dear."

Mr. Mills took her hand. "Emily, the five of us

are here on this very special day to reveal the truth about your father."

Her brow furrowed and she quaked inside. How could Mr. Mills know about her past? Tears welled in her eyes when she glanced at her aunt. "What is he talking about?"

"Sweetheart, your mother lied to you when you were a child. The fact was, your father went off to the service when you were four. He had always wanted children. It was my sister who didn't want you, but she loathed that your dad went into the Army and she vowed he would never see you again. Oh, he fought the system to try to get at least visitation rights, but the lawyer who drew up the documents made sure there were no stones unturned, so your mother won. She even got child support with no visitation rights."

That was impossible. "Auntie, the legal system wouldn't allow that to happen."

Ruby patted her hand. "I know it's hard to believe and that's what I thought too. But somehow the judge on the case allowed it." Ruby looked down. "I think your mom gave him… favors."

"What?" This couldn't be true. She'd lived with the guilt her mother instilled in her all those years ago making her think she was the reason he left? How could a mother do that to a child? "My daddy wanted me?"

Ruby nodded. "Yes, he did and does. After he got out of the Army, he went to law school. He wanted to protect others from the hand the legal system dealt him. You're a chip off the 'ole block since you want to be a lawyer someday."

A lawyer? Her father was a lawyer? Now she understood why she was always interested in law. She *was* like him.

Continuing, Ruby said, "He vowed to me no matter what, he'd always take care of you. And, honey, he has."

Her breath caught in her throat, her head spun and she felt weak. She sat back on the couch. The reassuring pat Zeb gave her did little to settle the raw emotions she felt at that moment. She inhaled a deep breath and glanced at Brittany who nodded and smiled like someone who was about to burst.

"Are you okay, dear?"

She forced herself to sit forward and realized Mr. Mills still held her hand. She was grateful for his added strength. "I'm not, but I am, if that makes any sense."

"Shall I go on then?"

"Yes, please." Everything may as well get out in the open so she wouldn't have any more wonders or doubts. After all, she was a grown woman and, since the Randle situation, she should be able to endure anything.

"After your mother died, there was still no way around the legalities, but those papers said I couldn't tell you who or where he was, and he could have no contact with you. They *didn't,* however, say *I* couldn't have contact with him. Soooo, he sent me money to help pay for your every need. You know those vacations we went on all those times?"

Emily's chin fidgeted and she blinked back tears that threatened to spill. She couldn't find her voice so she nodded.

"Well, he sent us on those trips. In return, I would give him updates on how you were doing and sent him pictures of every vacation and event you participated in at school and a lot more."

It was time she got herself together. However, this was all so overwhelming no matter how she'd dreamed of this day and what might happen when it arrived. This was reality and it was happening on her 25th birthday just like it said it could in the legal papers. "Okay, it's time I learned this man's name." Mr. Mills squeezed her hand and she met his gaze then heard his voice shakily say the words.

"It's Bob. His name is Bob."

Truth hit her as she looked into eyes the same color as hers, but she didn't speak. She glanced at Brittany and Mrs. Mills. They both had tears streaming down their face. Once again she turned her attention to Bob Mills. Could it be? She remembered the times she wished her and Brittany could trade places so she'd have a father like him. Now–. Her voice came out a whisper. "You're my... my..."

"I am, baby girl. I've dreamed of this day so many times. I love you, Emily, and always have."

How she'd longed to hear those words. He loved her! Her heart soared with happiness and she couldn't slow its rhythm, nor did she want too. She heard Brittany stand and she followed her lead. No matter how weak her knees were, she was going to hug the younger woman.

"Hey, sis, welcome to the family!"

Sis? Wait, they were really sisters! She released the hug and stared unbelievingly into her sister's eyes. Why hadn't she noticed the resemblance before? Oh, well, now was what counted. "Hey, did you know about this all along?"

"Nope. Just found out today. Mom and Dad were afraid I'd spill the beans. And you know me, I probably would have."

Bob Mills stood. "I'd love to have a big 'ole hug from my firstborn. If you don't mind that is."

This was all happening so fast she could barely breathe, but the joy that overwhelmed her was glorious. "Yes, sir, I'd love a hug." When he took her in his arms, she couldn't stop tears of delight and awe from flowing freely down her cheeks. A family. She had a family.

Zeb wanted to give the Mills', Emily and her aunt time to bond before he sprung his surprise gift on her. She'd probably had enough for the day, but this was something he needed to do.

Maybe, just maybe it would lend her the strength to overcome her fear of horses. Then he wanted to ask her to spend the rest of her life with him on the ranch.

When she told him not to call her so she could move on with her life, it cut him to the core. He heeded her wishes. However, he refused to give up on their love. Losing her was not something he would do. He'd lost one woman he thought he was in love with, but now, as sad as it was, he knew what he felt for Jasmine wasn't true love. His heart screamed to be with Emily for the rest of his life and he was going to do his best to fight for her.

He watched while Emily started to mingle with

the other guests. She was radiant. Happiness beamed from her eyes all the way down to her toes. Damn, he loved that woman and she loved him too whether she knew it or not. It was time.

Cell phone in hand, Zeb dialed Isom's number. In only two rings the man answered. He was outside waiting for the call. "Okay, you can bring her in."

"You sure you want to bring it inside?"

"I think it would be easier than bringing everyone out there. It shouldn't take long so come on in.

"You got it, Blue."

Emily was only a few feet away when he approached her and touched her elbow. "Could I borrow you for a minute?"

"Of course."

Noticing Ruby watching them, he nodded at her. He'd told her of the surprise earlier and she and Brittany wanted to be there when he gave it to Emily. The two women joined them at the door of the conference room. When Zeb heard the knock, he opened the door and there she stood, perfect in every way as Isom walked the small foal into the room.

Emily's first instinct was to run, but her heart immediately fell in love with the sweet face of the adorable little creature. Its nose was soft when it nuzzled her hand for attention and it surprised her when she didn't want to recoil at the warmth.

"Happy Birthday, Em."

"Oh, Zeb, I can't accept this from you?"

"Why not?"

"Well, b-because, ah…"

"That's what I thought. There's no reason."

She had to think of something. When the little thing was full grown, she'd be terrified of it. "Um, I don't have any place to put it."

"*It*, is a her. A filly." He put his arm around Emily's waist. "You can keep her at the ranch, but you'll have to come take care of her every day."

Brittany stepped up beside them. "Oh, isn't she precious? What are you going to name her, Sis?"

"I… ah."

"Why, what's wrong, dear? I've never known you to be speechless before. Don't you just love this little thing?" Ruby bent to pet the foal.

"She's, well, she's adorable, but Auntie, you know–"

"Oh, stop it, Emily Ann, this baby isn't going to hurt you."

The foal's soft nose nuzzled her hand again and she couldn't stop herself from petting her. Zeb stood, took the reins from Isom and handed it to her. Her heart skipped, but she took the leather straps.

"Why don't you take her over and sit down. Get on her same level and y'all get to know each other."

By this time, everyone in the room was gathered around and were making over the foal. Emily knew she couldn't blatantly say no and somehow, she didn't want to. The little thing wasn't any bigger than a large dog. Her pulse began to slow as she walked the tiny horse to the couch.

When Emily sat down, the foal put her nose on her shoulder, nibbled on her ear then rubbed her cheek against Emily's. It was so gentle, and the warmth of its breath made her giggle. "She's so sweet!"

Zeb sat next to her. "See, nothing to be afraid of."

"But when she grows up–"

"She'll still be just as sweet and gentle."

Emily swallowed the lump in her throat. Now her heart raced because of Zeb's closeness. The unique spice of his aftershave made her remember their time in the cabin and the way she felt in his arms when they danced. Could it be the gift he'd given her was the key to their happiness together?

Zeb took the reins from her and handed it to Isom. "You'd better take her out before she has an accident. We wouldn't want to have to clean up a mess."

The foal pushed its nose under Emily's hand like a puppy demanding to be petted. Everyone laughed, but Zeb's hearty laughter made her the happiest. The entire evening had been perfect. Her co-workers, her new family, Zeb and her little… "Hope," she said as she watched the man and filly walk out the door.

"What, dear?" Ruby asked.

She looked into Zebulon's eyes and his love was evident. "Her name is Hope."

EPILOGUE

Emily turned onto the driveway to the ranch. She stepped out of her car and took in the beauty of the landscape and her surroundings. The place would always hold a special corner of her heart.

It was the first time she'd been back, after the Randle incident, since she got her things and moved into her new apartment. She had decided, no matter how much she loved Hope she would never be comfortable around the horse when it was bigger. Telling Zeb was going to be hard, but saying goodbye to the filly would break her heart.

Zeb would try to talk her out of it, but she was determined to give the expensive gift back. She only wished she could give her love for him back, but it was something she'd keep for the rest of her life. Too bad she'd never get over her fear of horses, and all because of one evil man named Able Collins. It was hard to believe Randle confessed to the man's murder, but Zeb was smart enough to record it.

She would always be grateful for his intervention. The police and Texas Rangers were there, but Zeb had taken on the task of saving her on his own. He was a hero in her eyes and she was proud he'd decided to take his position back as a Ranger. He loved it so much and it would give him something to do besides think of her. *If* she ever crossed his mind like he did hers. She shook the thought. It was time to get this over with.

When she approached the front door she realized the dogs hadn't greeted her when she arrived. That was strange. Zeb's truck was there, but Isom's wasn't. "Buck? Earl?"
Silence.

Glancing around, she noticed a note on the front door. She stepped up onto the porch and read it out loud. "Isom, you can take the weekend off. I'm going to ride out to the cabin and do some fishing. Was hoping Emily would come see Hope this weekend so I moved her to the front stall, but haven't heard from Em so guess not. Thanks, Buddy, see you Monday."

"Damn! I should have called." She knew it would be impossible to get Zeb on his cell because there was no reception at the cabin. If he had moved Hope to the first stall in the barn, maybe she could get the courage up to go inside to see her. Could she do it by herself? She didn't know but she was going to try.

If she said her goodbye's to the horse now, she wouldn't have to be face to face with Zeb when she told him she wasn't going to accept his gift. It would be easier to have that conversation over the phone.

Getting closer to the large outbuilding, she drew in a deep breath and tried to calm her racing heart. This was something she had to do. She forced herself to take the first step inside the barn, then stood there for only a minute before she slowly walked down the breezeway toward the first stall. With every step, she reminded herself the horses couldn't get out. *It's okay, Emily, you can do this... you can do this... you can do this.*

When she reached the gate going into the cubicle she thought she'd be able to see the foal through the fencing but she wasn't there. Emily opened the gate to look inside. "Oh, no!" Hope lay on the hay-covered ground. Something was wrong with her, she wasn't moving! She had to act fast to save the little thing. Zeb, she had to go get Zeb!

Instinct took over and she ran to the tack wall, grabbed a bridle and bit, took it to the stall next to Hopes and managed to figure out how to put it on. She realized this was probably Hopes mother. "Girl, our baby's in trouble, we've got to get help!"

A thick blanket hung on a rack and the saddle rested on a stand nearby. Her focus was on her task and nothing else. She only hoped she could figure out how to put it on and fasten it. She remembered being told as a child to show the horse the blanket and saddle before you placed them on their back. This way they'd know what to expect.

With the blanket in place, she lifted the saddle from the stand. It was heavier than she thought it would be. With all her might, she heaved the leather contraption onto the horses back, making sure the horn was toward the front. She pulled the cinch as tight as she could, buckled them and made sure the saddle was secure. "I'm afraid that's as good as it's going to get."

She led the horse down the breezeway and outside. Getting to Zeb and back to help the filly was the only thing on her mind. She put her foot in the stirrup and hoisted herself onto the saddle. "Let's go, Momma!"

Horse hooves pounding the ground in a run drew Zeb's attention. Fear leaped into his heart when he saw Emily atop the mare. She was on a horse! Something had to be terribly wrong to force her to ride. He stood, dropped the fishing pole and ran in her direction.

"Zeb! Come quick! Something's wrong with Hope." Emily reined the mare to a halt.

"What happened?" He started toward the stallion he had tethered to the railing around the cabin porch.

"I don't know. I read your note and decided to try my courage and go see her. When I got there she was lying down and having trouble breathing."

He mounted his horse. It didn't sound good. "Are you okay?"

"Yes, I'm fine. I just want to get back and help her." She took off in a gallop. "Let's hurry, please!"

He didn't want to tell her the reason he asked if

she was alright was because she rode a horse to come get him. Did she even realize what she'd done? It was like her fear was pushed aside and it was second nature for her to be on the horse's back. He couldn't figure it out but now wasn't the time. His first concern was Hope.

When they approached the barn, Zeb took a running leap off his ride and hurried inside. If his suspicions were correct, the filly probably had pneumonia and that could be fatal. He heard Emily's footsteps coming up fast behind him when he reached the stall.

"What's wrong with her?"

"I don't know yet."

The gate unlatched, he opened it and rushed inside. His heart filled with happiness when he saw the foal standing there looking happy to see him. She didn't look in distress, but healthy and fit. He smiled. "I don't think anything's wrong with her."

"What are you talking about? She was down, Zeb." Emily pushed past Zeb.

Zeb's laughter infuriated her. How could he laugh at a time like this? When she elbowed her way around him, she stood there knowing her mouth was agape.

"Baby horses do sleep you know."

Tears welled in her eyes and spilled onto her cheeks. She fell to her knees and hugged the small animal around the neck. "You mean she was sleeping? Nothing was wrong?"

"That's what it looks like to me." He knelt down beside her.

"Oh, Hope! I'm so glad you're okay. You scared me!" She stroked Hope's soft nose and couldn't keep her hands off of her. Zeb's deep voice was just above a whisper.

"You don't know, do you?"

She gazed into the beautiful blue eyes she'd come to love. Butterflies! Not again. He was so close and his breath was like a gentle breeze warming her lips. "Know what?" The huskiness in her voice was almost embarrassing. Did he know how much she missed him?

"What Hope did for you?"

Unable to back away from the invisible hold he had on her, all she could do was shake her head.

"She made you ride, Em. When you feared for her life, you rode to get me."

Realization struck her. She'd gotten on a horse without thinking twice. She threw her arms around his neck and they tumbled into the hay. Her squeal came out louder than she'd intended. "Oh, Zeb! I rode a horse. A real live horse!" His arms felt wonderful around her.

"That you did."

Faster than a flash of lightning, Zeb's lips met hers. Never had she been kissed like that. She didn't want the storm it caused inside her to end but when it did, he planted tiny kisses up and down her neck. His warm breath in her ear made her shiver.

"Em?"

At that moment she felt so alive. "Mm-hmm." She didn't want the magic to stop.

"You know what this means, don't you?"

She missed his full embrace when he turned her

onto her back and hovered over her. "No?" It was a question, but did she want the answer?

"That's what you can't say."

Now she was getting confused. "What do you mean?" Why didn't he just shut up and kiss her again?

"There is no reason now for you to say no." He got up then knelt to one knee then pulled her to a sitting position.

Hope rested her small head on her shoulder. She loved this baby horse and she loved the cowboy in front of her. Denial of both was in the past. Zeb placed a gentle kiss on her lips then backed away.

"Em, you know I'm a Texas Ranger again, right?"

"Yes, and I'm so proud for you. I know how much you love the rangers." What did that have to do with saying no?

"I do love the rangers, but you should know something else."

His eyes reached so far into hers she wondered if he could actually see her affection. The love she had for this man couldn't be contained in her heart. It overflowed into her blood, her mind, body and soul. His words made her the happiest woman in the world.

"I love you, too. I love you more than life. You're on my mind day and night. What happened here today is the reason you can't say no." He took her hands in his. "Emily Tipton, will you marry me?"

THE END

ABOUT THE AUTHOR

Sharon Kizziah-Holmes started writing songs in her teens. She became an accomplished, professional musician. She and her husband spent eight years on tour where she entertained throughout the lower forty-eight states, Alaska and Canada, and performed with names like Willie Nelson, Hank Williams Jr., Faron Young and more.

In the 1990 Sharon and her husband moved to the Ozarks. They continued to play music in the area until 1996, but it was in 1992 when her passion changed from music to writing fiction. She joined Ozarks Romance Authors and was introduced to a whole new world.

Attending conferences, seminars and workshops to hone her skills, she learned the fundamentals of the mechanics of both the writing and publishing industries. Sharon began to share her knowledge with new and seasoned writers in workshops of her own.

While helping others learn the craft of writing and how to become published, she started her own indie assist company. In her career as an indie author publishing coordinator and service provider, she has helped over 60 authors publish over 300 books. Several of those authors have become best sellers.

Sharon Kizziah-Holmes is the co-founder, co-owner and CEO of A&S Holmes, Inc and its subsidiaries. Some of which are Paperback Press, The Recording Shop and The Barber Shop. She is currently President of Ozarks Romance Authors, Vice President of Sleuths' Ink Mystery Writers, a member of Springfield Writers Guild and Ozarks Writers League and has served five consecutive years as a chair-person for the American Cancer Society's SWMO Cattle Baron's Ball.

To see more of Sharon's books click, Sharon Kizziah-Holmes Author Page